Never Broke Up

Kiana Morrison

Contents

Chapter 1

P ast

I sat there, my heart pounding, as the ambulance screeched to a stop, and the paramedics swung the doors open. They rolled him out on a stretcher, and for a moment, I lost my grip on his hand.

Without thinking, I scrambled down and clung to his lifeless right hand, my fingers desperate to hold on. My cry of anguish pierced the sterile hospital air, echoing down the hallway as the nurses pushed the gurney forward.

They pleaded with me to release his hand but I couldn't bring myself to do it. I couldn't let go, it was my lifeline. I stole glances at his face, over and over, praying for his eyelids to flutter open, for his voice to break the silence just once.

The nurse blocked my way, refusing to let me in. Still, I couldn't tear my eyes away from him, my gaze locked on his fading figure until the doors closed."Please, Lord, just this one time, please let him make it, please." I pleaded through tears, my hands stained with blood as I clutched them together, sinking to the floor.

My hair clung to my skin, drenched in sweat, and the stench of blood enveloped me, but I couldn't care less. Not now. Not when the guy I love fought for his life inside

those hospital doors.

PresentI blinked and found myself in darkness. Pushing myself upright on the bed, i surveyed the room. That night, it still clung to me, haunting my dreams and

invading my thoughts, whether it was day or night. Its memories remained vivid, refusing to fade.My gaze shifted to the window, where raindrops danced upon the glass. "How did I forget to close it?" I whispered to myself. Tossing the white covers aside, I swung my legs over the edge of the bed.

The cold tile beneath my feet sent a shiver through me, and the cool breeze brushed against my exposed skin as I walked over to the window.With a determined pull, I closed the curtains, shutting out the world outside.I turned, preparing to return to the bed, hoping to escape the relentless memories of that haunting night.I cast a glance at the lamp stand and flicked it on. I had never been the type to sleep in darkness, but that changed one fateful night, a night etched into my memory.

I reached for my phone, its screen illuminating the room with a soft gl ow.It read 3 AM. I sighed and slid back into my bed, pulling the covers tightly around me. I knew what was coming-the same haunting dream, once more.ThadMy legs moved smoothly on the treadmill as I ran, fingers reaching for my Air Pods. With a double tap, I activated them."Yes?" My deep voice echoed in the otherwise silent gym."Mr. Whitlock, I've tried speaking to the clients repeatedly, but they're still refusing our offer," my assistant's voice resonated through the Air Pods.I sighed, the weight of the business on my shoulders. "Alright, Schedule another appointment with them for lunch today. I should be in the office in..." I paused to check my wristwatch, "an hour and a half," I concluded."But sir, we have a meeting with the head of resources for the upcoming...""Cancel it," I interrupted without hesitation."Okay, sir," he responded, and the call ended.I removed my Air Pods and brought the treadmill to a stop, stepping off it.Grabbing my phone and towel, I made my way out of the gym, wiping away the sweat that had gathered on my neck and forehead.

SeraphinaMy phone's insistent buzzing jarred me awake, and I groaned while reaching for it, stubbornly keeping my eyes shut."Hello," I rasped, my voice hoarse from sleep."Seraphina!!" Clara's enthusiastic yell caused me to yank the phone away from my ear for a moment.

Good morning," I mumbled, choosing to ignore her spirited greeting."W here are you? Do you even know what time it is right now? I get that you're a top chef here, but shouldn't you still be here, huh?" She playfully complained, her tone a mix of concern and jest.I opened my eyes, immediately assaulted by the bright sunlight streaming in through the curtains."I'm taking a leave today, Clara. I won't be coming to the restaurant," I said,

sitting up in bed."What the heck... why didn't you tell me?" Her voice carried a hint of disappointment, and I could sense she'd miss my prese nce."I'm sorry. I only decided last night," I explained."Lucky you. But I'm not jealous, don't think I am, because I'm also a chef, just like you. Bye... for now," she said before abruptly ending the call.I chuckled as I looked at my phone. Clara was exactly the kind of friend I needed in my life, always there to boost my spirits and give me the energy to

face the day.A smile curled on my lips as I let out a long breath, taking in the sunlight that now flooded my room with warm rays. I'd dreamt about it once more. But,

well, I suppose I had grown accustomed to these recurring dreams.

They were now a familiar part of my life. My eyes widened in alarm as I glanced at the time; it was already past 11 AM."Oh God! Sera, what's wrong with you?" I chided myself, a surge of panic compelling me to spring out of bed and rush towards the bathroom.

ThadI sat there, observing the lady as she spoke, her finger repeatedly pressing the button to advance her presentation.

A throbbing headache gripped my head, prompting a soft groan as I instinctively adjusted my tie."I think we should concentrate on expanding our digital presence. Market trends clearly indicate a rising demand for online services, and we should seize that opportunity," her voice contin ued."That's a valid point. Digital expansion is crucial, but I believe we've made strides in that area, haven't we? Any other suggestions?" I finally interjected,

breaking the silence that had enveloped the vast hall.

"I believe we should tailor our services to specific client segments. By understanding their unique needs, we can offer more personalized solutions,"

a man on my right proposed, his gaze fixed on me."Elaborate," I replied, adjusting my tie once more."Perhaps we should also explore strategic par tnerships.Collaborating with

complementary businesses could help us reach new markets and clients more efficiently," he suggested."Any specific sectors you have in mind for potential partnerships?" I inquired, drumming my fingers lightly on the table."Well, I've compiled a list of...""You should send that to my office," I interrupted him and rose from my chair.They promptly stood up, bowing

I sighed as I made my way out of the meeting, the weight of stress pressing down on me.

"Is the car ready?" I asked my assistant as we entered the elevator."Yes, sir. The clients will be there in an hour," he replied, checking his wristwatch.I nodded and retrieved my phone, noticing a new message."How are you doing darling? Hope you are not too stressed?" - mumI sighed, my fingers tapping out a reply.I am stressed, and I can feel it. But I can't give up on the company. I know how long it took me to bring it to where it is now, and all I want is to take it even further.

Seraphina"Luna," I squealed with delight as I spotted my dog in her cage. She bounded out and rushed toward me, her tail wagging with joy.I grinned and crouched down to pet her.

"You've gotten fatter without me,

haven't you? Didn't you miss me, huh?" I teased, gently shaking her before gathering her into my arms."I'm so glad you're safe now. I can't imagine you having another bout of food poisoning," I said with relief as I secured her with a seatbelt and closed the

car door.

I circled around and settled into the driver's seat, fastening my own seatbe lt.As I started the car, my phone rang from my coat pocket, and I retrieved it to

answer the call.

"Hello."

"Sera, you're coming to the event this Saturday, right? I know you're a very busy person, and you value your time a lot, but we really need the experts to be there," my manager's voice came through the phone."But I thought it was postponed?" I inquired."Well, that's what we were told, but they just called this morning to inform us about the event happening this Saturday. Will you be available?" she asked."Of course, I'll be there.""Thank you so much, Sera. You don't know how much this means to us," she expressed her gratitude, and I smiled.We exchanged goodbyes, and I ended the call. "Too much for being a top expert chef, right, Luna?" I remarked, glancing at my dog.My phone buzzed once more, and a smile crept onto my face as I glanced at the caller ID."Senior," I greeted."When will you stop calling me that, Sera?" His deep voice boomed from the

other end."When I wish to," I replied, teasingly."You picked up Luna from the hospital today, right? Let's celebrate it tonight,"

he suggested.He always remembered even the little things, didn't he?

I can't believe you remembered.""Why wouldn't I? I'll buy a cake; you should let Luna know," he said, laughter lacing his words."Okay, I'll be expecting you," I agreed before ending the call."It seems you'll be getting a cake tonight, Luna," I said with a grin, glancing at my dog, who now had her eyes closed.I chuckled and continued on my way.ThadI parked my car in the garage and switched off the engine. Stepping out of the vehicle, I carefully removed my suit jacket, holding it in my hands.As I closed the door behind me, I was greeted by the unexpected sight of lights illuminated throughout the house.

The maids should have already left for the day, and they typically ensured the lights were turned off. I couldn't help but wonder who had turned them on.

With a sense of curiosity, I made my way gently toward the living room. Soft sounds emanated from the kitchen, drawing my attention. I sighed and placed my suit jacket on the couch before proceeding further.

Standing at the entrance to the kitchen, my hands stuffed into my pants pockets, I observed Callista. Her auburn hair was pulled up, and she wore gloves on her hands

She was struggling with frying something, taking a step back whenever the oil sparked up. It was evident that cooking wasn't her usual activity.

"What are you doing, Callie?" I asked, my deep voice shattering the house silence, apart from the sounds of her cooking.

She turned, alarmed at the

sound of my voice, and smiled."You scared me, Thad. I didn't hear you come in," she admitted, then returned her attention to her cooking.I sighed, growing impatient, and approached her. "I said, what are you doing?" I repeated, my frustration evident.

I was already tired of watching

her struggle."I'm cooking... for you," she replied with a hint of defiance.I reached out, taking her hands and removing the gloves before switching off the gas. I placed them on the counter and turned to face her.

"What was that for, Thad?" She asked, her voice laced with surprise and confusion."Whatever you think it is, Callie. You can't just come to my house and start cooking at this time of the day. It's past 9 PM," I stated firmly, looking into her eyes."But I was trying to cook for you. You seem tired, and..." she started to explain, her voice trailing off."You don't need to do that for me, Callie. You're a friend, not a maid. The maids have already finished their work and left. You don't need to cook for me," I interrupted her, my tone resolute.She sighed, and I could see a flicker of hurt in her eyes. "I... I'm sorry.

I didn't know it would make you uncomfortable. I was just trying to make things easier for you," she apologized softly.

"It already is, Callie. All I need you to do is grab your bag; I'll drop you off," I said, moving to walk past her.

However, she was quick to grab my right wrist, halting my steps."You don't need to do that. I can go home myself; I brought my car," she said softly, walking past me."Okay," I replied quietly, trailing behind her as she headed to the living room to retrieve her handbag. "Have a good night's rest, Thad," she whispered in a hurt tone, her smile forced, and it was clear to me. "You too," I responded as she nodded and left.

Hi Readers, this is the first chapter of my book, it is actually longer than this but I had to cut it short. What do you think of this?

Chapter 2

Seraphina

"Cheers," I chimed in, clinking my glass against Lysander's. His blue eyes sparkled with a smile.

I took a sip of my beer and cast a glance at Luna, who was asleep beside me.

Even though this celebration was for her, it didn't feel quite like one.

"It's been a while since we've sat down like this to drink, Senior," I remarked, setting my cup on the dining table before looking up at him.

He nodded in agreement.

"You know, you didn't have to buy a cake for Luna. It's a waste of money," I commented, expressing my concern.

"Why are you worried about that? Luna isn't even complaining," he remarked, glancing at my contented dog.

I couldn't help but smile at Luna's peaceful demeanor.

"How's work treating you? Are you still planning on quitting?" he inquired, his curiosity evident. I nodded in response.

"I've thought about it, and I've made up my mind. I'm going to quit and travel the world until I get tired of it. I've made and saved up enough money for that," I explained, with a chuckle.

"This year. I plan to do it this year and take a break," I continued, and he nodded, understanding my decision.

"Just do it as long as it makes you happy," he encouraged.

"This should be your mantra now, Lys, always do what makes me happy. You say that all the time," I teased, taking another sip of my beer.

"Because I mean it," he replied with a sincere smile, making me smile in return.

"Are you busy this Saturday? I want to treat you to lunch," he asked, his proposal catching me off guard.

"Lunch? Out of the blue?" I questioned, genuinely surprised.

"Yeah. My business is booming very fast lately, Sera, and we should celebrate it... together," he explained, reclining in his chair.

I sighed and considered his offer. "Let's make it dinner, Senior. I have an event to attend, and I'll be busy by then."

Event? You're going out to work again?" he asked, a hint of concern in his voice, and I nodded in confirmation.

"It's a top-tier event, and they need the experts there. Though I'll be in the kitchen, behind the scenes as always," I explained, which elicited a laugh from

him. "But they need me, and I need the paycheck too."

He smiled in understanding. "Okay then. Dinner it is," he agreed, and we shared a laugh, the ease of our friendship evident.

Thad

I took a seat at the table, maintaining a calm demeanor as I watched the violinists expertly craft melodies with their nimble fingers.

The opulent hall

was brimming with high-status individuals, a mix of business magnates, accomplished women, and influential partners, all engaged in animated conversations and soaking in the exquisite atmosphere.

Sighing softly, I cast my eyes around the room, then retrieved my phone to check my emails. The lavish party had been in full swing for approximately two hours, a lavish affair that had treated us to a succession of delectable

dishes.

My attention drifted to the eighth course before me, marveling at the meticulous presentation that exuded professionalism.

As my phone buzzed, I excused myself from the table and retreated to the balcony to answer the call.

"Yes?" I responded.

"Mr. Whitlock, the clients are on their way to the event," my assistant reported.

"I successfully persuaded them to accept our invitations and outlined the benefits they stand to gain from attending."

I couldn't help but chuckle lightly as I gazed down at the lively crowd outside, all caught up in their merriment.

"Well done, Mark. You really pulled it off," I complimented him before ending the call.

Returning to my table, I noticed a chef already hard at work. I took a seat, mentally preparing to persuade my clients who would arrive shortly.

My phone buzzed, and I promptly replied to the message. Laughter and gasps from a neighboring table caught my attention, prompting me to turn and see

what was going on.

Standing there was a lady in a chef's attire and a cap. She expertly fried her dish with remarkable speed, adding little tricks that left the guests at her table both surprised and delighted. Despite her outfit, she exuded a simple yet elegant charm.

However, my throat went dry when she looked up, revealing

her captivating emerald green eyes, deep and beautiful.

A strange sense of familiarity washed over me. She felt like an old friend, though I couldn't quite place where we might have crossed paths.

I struggled to tear my gaze away, but it remained fixed on her as I watched in fascination,

unable to look away, as she worked her culinary magic with graceful ease.

She wrapped up her cooking show and explained her dish to the impressed guests. But my eyes remained locked on her, particularly her captivating

emerald eyes that never met mine.

When she finished, she walked past my table, and her delightful cologne wafted by, oddly familiar.

Why did her scent make me so strangely happy? Why do i feel this way? It felt like I'd encountered it before.

Lost in thought, I hadn't noticed how long I'd been staring at her departure until I felt a tap on my shoulder.

I turned to

see my assistant beside me, giving me a quizzical look.

"Mr. Whitlock, the..." My assistant's voice faded as my head suddenly blanked out, a pounding sensation throbbing through my skull.

I let out a low groan,

unable to focus. Closing my eyes briefly, I reopened them to find myself entranced by those mesmerizing green eyes once more.

The pain in my head

intensified, forcing me to gently push my assistant away and hastily rise from my seat, heading for the nearest bathroom.

I slammed the bathroom door behind me, my head still throbbing. Gasping for air, I leaned on the sink, my heart racing much faster than usual.

What was happening to me? Why this strange mix of excitement and fear?

"What is it called babe?"

"Tangled."

"Tangled?. I love the smell, it smells so much like you"

I groaned as a sudden memory, one I didn't even know existed, flooded my mind. It was a memory of a guy and a girl, my voice, my own fucking voice.

I was sitting on a bed, and someone was beside me, but their face remained frustratingly blurry.

I slumped down to the floor, clutching my head. What was happening to me?

Seraphina

"Sera, you don't know how much this means to me. I just suddenly had a number 2, and I couldn't hold it in anymore," Clara said, hugging me tightly as I changed into my outfit.

"It's fine. I've done your job for you anyway," I replied with a smile.

That's why you're the best friend ever. Did the guests ask about why I left, huh?" Clara inquired, gripping my arms.

I shook my head and sighed. "No, Clara. They did not ask me about you for once," I replied.

"I knew they wouldn't. You've charmed them with your skills, huh?" She teased, making me chuckle.

"I'm leaving now. I have a dinner with someone," I explained, grabbing my handbag. But she quickly blocked my path.

"Dinner? With who?" Clara inquired.

"Who do you think it is?" I replied calmly, and she gasped.

"It's a date. You're going on a blind date, Sera," she exclaimed, making me quickly cover her mouth with my right hand to shush her.

"God, Clara, your voice is so loud. It's not a blind date; it's a dinner with Lys," I clarified.

"Lys? That handsome guy of yours with golden hair and ocean eyes?" She asked, pulling my hand away.

I nodded. "It's more like sapphire blue, though," I added.

"Who cares if it's ocean or sapphire? They make me want to drown in them," she said, hugging herself slightly.

I chuckled as I made my way past her.

"Good night, Clara," I replied, waving my hand.

Goodnight! Get home safe and be careful with that handsome dude!" she yelled, making me quicken my pace as I left.

Thad

I looked at my bloodshot eyes in the mirror, adjusting my tie and suit. After taking a deep breath, I headed back to the hall.

Approaching my table, I noticed a lady dressed in red with her auburn hair neatly tied up.

"Callic?" I said as I sat down.

She looked up from her phone and smiled upon seeing me.

"Thad."

"You didn't tell me you would be here," I remarked.

"I wanted to make it a surprise. Are you shocked?" She said with a laugh, and i couldn't help but chuckle.

"I also received an invitation to this event," Callista said, and I nodded.

"Thad, about that night I came to your house unannounced... I'm really sorry..." Callista began, but I couldn't focus on her words as I spotted the same chef i had seen earlier.

She was now wearing a brown coat and looked quite different from before. An inexplicable urge to approach her, like an old friend, surged within me.

Without a second thought, I sprang up from my chair and glanced down at Callie, who appeared confused by my sudden

action.

"Thad, what's wrong...?"

I just remembered that I left something in my car. I need to go and get it. I'll be right back," I interrupted her and swiftly made my way toward the

entrance.

I stepped outside and was greeted by the chilly night breeze. Spotting her not far away, I hurriedly walked in her direction. However, my steps halted abruptly when I observed her approach a car and get inside.

Glancing at the

driver's seat, I saw a man seated there, engaged in conversation with her. A sharp pain pierced my chest, causing me to audibly gasp as I watched the car

drive away, out of my sight.

"What the heck is happening to me? Why am I feeling this sadness? Why did

I even come out here?" I whispered, clutching my chest.

My phone buzzed suddenly, and I retrieved it with a shaky hand.

"Yes?" I croaked.

"Mr. Whitlock, the clients... they left. I tried to detain them and explain some things, but they departed before I could do anything," my assistant's voice

echoed, carrying a sense of urgency.

I let out a sigh of relief as the pain in my chest gradually subsided.

"It's fine, Mark. I will take care of it," I assured him before ending the call.

"Thad?"

I spun around to find Callista standing a few steps away, holding my car keys in front of me.

"You left your car keys on the table. You are so forgetful," she

teased as she approached me.

I sighed and took the keys from her, glancing in the direction where the car had disappeared before turning back to Callista.

"There's no need for it anymore. Let's go back inside," I told her.

Callista looked momentarily puzzled but then nodded in agreement.

We both headed back into the event hall, but my mind was consumed by one question.

Who is she? Who is the green-eyed lady who had turned my night into a chaotic mess?

Chapter 3

P ast"Where is he? Where is my son? Where is Thaddeus?" Vivienne's voice echoed through the hallway as she rushed toward me.

I sat on the floor, tears streaming down my face, unable to find the words to respond.

Her grip on my hands was strong, and I tried to convey what had happened, but my voice faltered. I wanted to tell her that he was in the theater room, caught between

the precipice of life and death, but the words wouldn't come out.

I could only sob, overwhelmed by the weight of the moment.

"I..." My voice was choked with sobs, rendering me incapable of speaking clearly.

Vivienne let go of my hands, stepping back, creating distance.

"You need to calm down, Mrs. Whitlock," Sean urged, holding her shoulders gently as he guided her to a nearby seat.

Her gasp echoed through the hallway, the sound mingling with her cries of anguish.

"I swear to God if anything happens to my son, I will shred you, Seraphina. I will," she yelled, her eyes locked onto me, filled with a mixture of desperation and anger.

I paused my sobs, my tear-filled eyes locking onto her gaze, those once-familiar gray eyes. But they were different now, void of any emotion. It was a stark contrast to the eyes I had seen countless times when visiting her at home, when sharing moments in the kitchen, or even during our shopping trips.

This look was chilling, as if she

harbored a desire to harm someone, perhaps even to harm me.

"Vivienne," I managed to croak, my voice hoarse, and took a tentative step towards her.

She rose from her seat and approached me, her finger pointing accusingly at my face.

"It's your fault. Everything is your fault, Sera. He apologized, didn't he? He did, but you still refused to listen. Now see where you've put my only son," she sobbed.

Her words cut through me like a knife. This wasn't the Vivienne I knew, the one who had always supported our relationship. Now, she felt distant, like a mother-in-law who disapproved of us.

At that moment, I experienced a feeling I had never felt before. It was as if the weight of the world had crushed me. I wished it was me on that operating table, undergoing the surgery.

I yearned to turn back time, to just a few hours ago, and change the course of events. I was overwhelmed with misery and guilt.PresentI groaned as the persistent buzzing of my phone pulled me from my slumber.Opening my eyes slowly, I stretched my arms and fumbled for my phone on the nightstand."Hello?" I mumbled sleepily."I know I told you not to always call me, but this is too much, Sera," my mom's voice scolded through the phone.I yawned and sat up in bed, Luna, my dog, eagerly joining me, her tail wagging in excitement."Good morning, Mum," I greeted, gently petting Luna's head."How are you doing, Sera? You can't keep me in the dark this way," she complained.

What do you mean, Mum?" I asked, not quite understanding her point ."Why didn't you tell me that Lys now works in your city? I phoned him this morning, and he said he's been in your city for over six months now."I sighed and climbed out of bed."Gosh, Mum, you scared me. Do I need to tell you every detail of Lysander's life?" I asked, pulling the curtains apart to let the morning light in."You should; he's like a son to me," she said, and I could sense the hint of a pout in her voice."How is retirement going for you, Mum? Do you need anything?" I asked, walking over to the mirror."I'm fine, Sera. I miss you, and I just wanted to hear your voice," she replied, making me chuckle."I knew that's the reason you called; you don't have to use Lys as an excuse," I teased."I have to go now, Mum. I have an outing today," "An outing? With who? Lys?" She asked.I groaned slightly. "Mum, please, let's not talk about that this morning. I'm going out with Luna, not Lys. He has his own life to live, Mum," I said firmly."When will you bring the right man home, Sera? It's been years now, and you're 26. You're not getting any younger. You need to move on from... what

happened," she persisted, and I could sense the direction of her speech."I have to go now. Bye, Mum!" I said, quickly ending the call before she could

reply.

I placed my phone on the table and looked at myself in the mirror.I sighed and glanced at the ring on the table, the one that I wore every day and everywhere I went. It had always been with me, and even though I knew he was somewhere in this world, moving on with his life, I still couldn't bring

myself to take it off.

So, I just kept on wearing it.

I picked up the ring and looked through it, memories flooding back.Past "Open it," he urged, his loving eyes fixed on me.

I smiled and opened the little black box, gasping as I saw a silver ring nestled inside.

"Thaddeus!" I whispered, tears welling up in my eyes.

"It's a couple's ring, I got it for us. See, I have mine too," he said, showing me his middle finger. "Do you like it?" Hope shone in his eyes.

"I love it, Thad. I've always wanted to have one with you," I whispered as I pulled out the ring and read aloud what was engraved on it.

"Your heart belongs to me," I said, and he smiled.

"It is true, isn't it?" He asked, seeking confirmation. I nodded in response.

"Put it on for me," I urged, extending my hand towards him. He chuckled as he picked up the ring and slid it onto my middle finger.

"Don't ever take this off, Sera. It means the world to me," he said, gazing at me with his deep grey eyes. I smiled and pulled him in for a kiss.

"I won't," I whispered against his lips, and he smiled, licking his own lips.

"Do you have to do that every time I kiss you?" I teased, lightly hitting his chest as I laughed.

"Yes, I will do it all the time," he said, wrapping his arms around my waist. I smiled and ran my fingers through his hair, tousling it a bit before wrapping my arms

around his neck.

"I love you, Seraphina. I really do," he whispered against my ear.I smiled as I felt tears trickle down my right cheek. I quickly wiped them away and placed the ring back on the table."What's wrong with you, Sera? You promised not to cry," I whispered to myself as I made my way to the bathroom.

ThadI sat down in my office, tapping my fingers lightly on my desk as I pondered the woman I had seen. I'm not usually one to be intrigued by women, having encountered many beautiful ones, but she was different.

There was something

about her that I couldn't quite place. Was it her eyes, or her skill in her profession?I sighed and decided to let it go. It was just a chance encounter, and I might never see her again. Just as I was lost in thought, I heard a knock on my office door and sat up straight."Come in," I called out.

Mark entered, holding his familiar pad and file in one hand."Mr. Whitlock, you have an appointment with the hotel architect. You are to

meet with him in the next two hours, sir," he said."Give me a minute, and I will be ready," I replied, standing up from my chair.He nodded before leaving my office.

Seraphina"Luna, wait. Stop running, oh God!" I called out in a breathless voice as I watched my energetic dog sprint ahead of me. She was overjoyed, as it had been a while since our last hill climbing adventure, while I struggled to keep pace.I finally gave in, coming to a panting halt, my chest heaving with exh austion.Luna continued her sprint and soon disappeared from my view. A few elderly couples strolled past, casting amused smiles my way, seemingly entertained by my inability to keep up with my lively companion.

Returning their smiles with a friendly nod, I decided to take a breather and knelt down to tie my shoelaces."Luna!" I hollered again, resuming my pursuit when I heard my phone vibrating in my pocket.

Retrieving my phone, a smile crept onto my face as I

glanced at the caller ID."Hello," I answered, my voice strained."Seraaa... hee... he..." Clara's voice trembled, choked with sobs on the other end of the phone.

My concern grew as I struggled to make sense of her words. "What happened, Clara? You need to calm down; I can't hear what you're saying," I urged,

anxiety mounting with her crying."Tyler... he cheated on me. I got a picture from someone, and I came to the hotel, and I saw him with a white-haired girl, and..." Her words trailed off into continued sobbing.I let out a sigh, trying to be the voice of reason in her moment of distress."W here are you?" I asked gently."Ivory Locks Hotel," she mumbled between sobs."Okay. I'm coming to get you, Clara. Please, don't do anything rash over there,

okay?" I reassured her before ending the call.As I desperately searched for Ivory Locks on the map, I couldn't help but mutter to myself, "Why does he have to cheat on her today of all days?"

My heart ached for Clara, and I felt a surge of empathy for the pain she must be going through.Once I located the hotel on the map, I realized it was a two-hour drive from my current location.

"She actually went that far to meet him? Oh my God!

Clara," I whispered, shaking my head in disbelief.Panicking about the distance and the urgency of the situation, I called for Luna, "Luna! Come out, we need to leave now!" I yelled, racing in the direction my dog had run off to.

Thad"I want this part to be taken down and the other side of it. You should do it in a way that won't affect the regular activity of the hotel right now" I said to the architect as I looked through the wall in front of me.I have always wanted to renovate this part of the hotel but I keep on

postponing it due to my schedules."We will take care of that sir. Is there anything else you need us to do?" The architect asked"No. That will be all, you should send the overview to my assistant before you start" I said, walking past him."Okay sir." He said behind me."What's next on my schedule John?" I asked my assistant."A meeting with the head of resources, you were suppose to meet with them but you told me to cancel it"he said. "Okay. Let's go" I said, as I made my way down the hall. Mark's phone rang and he spoke with whomever was on the phone before cutting the call."Mr Whitlock, i got a call now that I left a file back in there. I want to go back to get it quickly sir"he said making me to stop in my track."You forgot a file? That is so unlike you Mark"I said."I am sorry about that sir" he apologized."I will be waiting in the car"I said, and started walking away.

SeraphinaI parked my car in the hotel's crowded parking lot, leaving Luna inside with the windows slightly down for some fresh air. Bracing myself for what lay ahead, I slipped on my coat over the casual outfit I had worn earlier-just a

crop top and leggings from our hill climbing adventure.The opulence of the hotel struck me as I entered, with its grand lobby and well-dressed staff. I couldn't help but mutter to myself, "Tyler has got some money to come and lodge in a hotel like this?"

I made a beeline for the elevator, pressed the button for the 23rd floor, and ascended swiftly. Upon reaching my destination, I walked down the corridor to room 203. The door swung open, revealing a white-haired girl with a scowl etches across her face.So she actually exists."Uhm... Hi," I said awkwardly, trying to peer behind the white-haired girl to spot Clara."Who the hell are you?" She responded rudely, her expression hostile."Sera. My name is Sera, and I'm looking for Clara. Do you know if she is...""I don't know anyone by that name," she interrupted me abruptly and slammed

the door in my face."Wow. One would think I'm the one who got cheated on," I muttered sarcastically, shaking my head as I ran my hands through my hair in frustration.Just then, my phone buzzed, and I received a message from Clara, indicating that she was in the lodge. I let out a sigh, ready to continue my search for her.

"But she said room 203 earlier," I mumbled in frustration, clutching my phone tightly as I dialed Clara's number. As I continued down the corridor, my steps were slow and hesitant, my anxiety mounting.

Upon reaching the elevator, I pressed the button for the desired floor and waited impatiently for Clara to answer.

But the call went unanswered, leaving me with a sense of unease. I let out a weary sigh, folding my arms protectively around my chest.

Feeling the elevator's silence close in around me, I turned to check if I was alone. To my surprise, I discovered a man standing behind me, engrossed in his phone, his fingers tapping furiously on the screen.

He seemed oddly

familiar, though I couldn't quite place him.Suddenly, he looked up, and our eyes locked. My heart thundered in my chest, and a sense of recognition washed over me, even though I couldn't immediately identify him.

Chapter 4

As soon as I laid my eyes on him, my breath hitched in my throat. He stood there, draped in an impeccably tailored black suit that oozed expense.

His hair, meticulously gelled to the back, added an air of timeless charm to his already striking appearance.But it wasn't just his outward appearance that left me in awe, it was the way he looked at me. His grey eyes, seemed to pierce through the depths of my

soul.

It was a gaze that I could recognize anywhere in the world, a gaze that held a deep history between us.

Our eyes locked, and I felt an unexplainable surge of emotions welling up within me.

Tears threatened to spill from my eyes as his gaze held me captive."Why does he look so much like him? They look so alike."I turned my gaze away from him in a hurry, my finger finding the 21st floor button on the panel.

I just couldn't bring myself to stand next to someone who looked so much like him. The pain it stirred within me was too much to endure.I stepped out of the elevator and began to walk away, even though my legs felt like jelly beneath me. Finding a chair, I sank into it as tears welled up in my eyes.Why am I crying?" I wondered aloud, my trembling voice betraying my confusion.

I couldn't pinpoint the exact reason for my tears. Was it because seeing someone who resembled him brought back a flood of memories and emotions?"Ma'am, are you okay?"

A concerned female staff member asked as she looked down at me.

She kindly offered me a tissue, and I accepted it with a soft "thank you."T hadI watched as the elevator door closed, leaving me alone in the elevator.

The thumping in my heart grew louder, and for the second time in a week, I had

come face to face with those mesmerizing green eyes that always seemed to make me lose control.

I clutched my head as a sharp, searing pain shot through it, and I couldn't help but groan in agony.

My phone slipped from my grasp, falling to the ground.My head pounded relentlessly, as if it might split open at any moment.Weakness spread through my legs, and I began to hear voices in my head, their words echoing in a chaotic chorus."Why do you always look at me like that? Like you're peering into my soul?" a female voice questioned.

"Because you're beautiful," a deep voice replied with a hint of vibration, followed by hearty laughter.I let out an even louder groan as I collapsed to the elevator floor, the pounding in my head intensifying with each passing moment.

Seraphina"Clara!" I called out as I approached her in the lodge. She was seated there, her eyes swollen, and she nervously fiddled with her fingers." What took you so long? I've been waiting for you," she cried out, her voice trembling.

I hurriedly pulled her into a warm embrace."I'm sorry. I should have come sooner," I reassured her, gently patting her back as she clung to me, sobbing into my neck."He left me, Sera. He didn't apologize and said it was my fault. He..."

Her sobs grew stronger, and I held her even tighter."It's okay now. Stop crying," I whispered, pulling away from her and wiping the tears from her eyes."Why are your eyes red? Did you cry for me?" she inquired, and I managed a faint smile, finding her question slightly amusing."No, nothing like that. Just something got into my eyes. Let's go now; we're drawing too much attention here," I replied, glancing around as a few curious onlookers directed their gaze our way.

She nodded, retrieving her bag and standing up.

Thad"Mr. Whitlock, I've been trying to call you, but it wasn't going through. Are you okay, sir?" Mark inquired as soon as I approached my car.

His concern was evident, given my disheveled appearance. My hair was a mess from how i had clutched and squeezed it in the elevator, my tie was half undone, and my suit was wrinkled."Take me home, Mark," I requested, and he promptly held the car door open for me.

He could tell that I wasn't in the mood for any argument."Okay, sir," he replied, recognizing the need for a swift departure.I was seething with anger, though I couldn't quite explain why. It irked me that someone's mere presence had the power to make me lose control of myself, and the thought of it frustrated me to no end.

I couldn't shake the memory of the shock on her face, as if she knew me or was simply taken

aback by seeing me.My thoughts felt muddled, and exhaustion washed over me. All I wanted was to drift off to sleep, to escape the confusion of why I always reacted this way

upon setting my eyes on her and why she seemed so familiar.With a heavy sigh, I yanked my tie from around my neck and tossed it onto the chair beside me.

Chapter 5

P ast

"Mrs. Whitlock, just this once. Please, let me see him. I'm begging you," I pleaded desperately in front of his mother, her stern expression emphasizing the weariness in her swollen eyes.

Fear and worry gripped me, and I needed to know if he was okay, if he had woken up.I'd been sleeping outside the hospital for days, forming bonds with some of the nurses in the process.

Vivienne, however, adamantly denied my requests to see Thaddeus, and it tore at my heart.

My appetite had vanished, and I'd barely taken care of myself, only return-ing home once to change my blood-stained clothes.

"I told you, I don't want you anywhere near my son. Is that so hard for you to understand, Seraphina?" she yelled, frustration lacing her words.

"I'll do anything you ask, but please, don't push me away like this, Vivienne. Please," I pleaded through my sobs, but she remained unmoved. "Do you think I'm happy about how things have turned out? I'm not. But this is my son we're talking about, my only son. I've always supported your relation ship, but not when it's hurting him. You see, Seraphina, I've been scared for my son for a long time."

"What... what do you mean?" I stammered, tears trickling down my face to my chapped lips.

"I've been scared ever since Thad started having trouble sleeping if you weren't beside him. He was becoming obsessed with you, and you knew it!" She gritted out, her frustration and concern clear in her voice.

I swallowed hard, a lump forming in my throat as I wondered if her words held any truth.

"He wasn't," I whispered, but it felt feeble in the face of her accusations.

"You made him that way, Seraphina. That's why he's still in a coma. He hasn't opened his eyes. Do you know how badly I've yearned to see my son awake again? Let me make something clear - I'll ensure he never crosses paths with you again. I don't want a toxic girl like you near my son. So please, go as far away from us as you can. From Thaddeus," she yelled, her words cutting through me as she stormed past, brushing against my shoulder.

I slumped onto the cold floor outside the hospital, my life crumbling around me. I wanted to cry, but my eyes were dry, and my body felt devoid of strength. I just sat there, staring at the ground.

Everything had changed overnight, all because of a foolish mistake - not answering a phone call.

Present

I dropped my handbag onto the chair and slumped into it, letting out a heavy sigh. Luna wagged her tail and disappeared into another room while I got up to pour myself a glass of water from the jug in the dining area.

As I settled back into the chair, my phone buzzed with a message from Lys, asking if I would be available tomorrow. I replied with a simple "Yes" and then received a message from Clara.

"Thank you for showing up today, Sera," -Clara

I sent a reply and sighed once more as his face continued to haunt my thoughts.

How could he resemble him so much? I had left him in that city years ago.

Had he moved to this city? Was he really Thad? His mother had assured me that I'd never come across him again, so how was this happening?

I scrolled through my contacts, my finger hovering over a number I hadn't called in eight years. I wrestled with the decision of whether to dial it or not.

* * * Thad

I placed the last album of photos on the table in my study room and sighed, leaning back in my chair.

"Who the heck is she?" I whispered, my gaze fixed on the door.

I had scoured through all the photos, desperately searching for a green-eyed girl, but there wasn't a single image of her, not one.

It was as if she had never been a part of my life. I couldn't shake the curiosity about who she was and why she was stirring up such emotions in me.

Had she been someone from before the accident I had years ago? But my mother had assured me that I didn't forget anyone close to me. So who was she?I ran my hand through my hair, trying to remember if I had dated or known her during college, but my memory failed me. I had never seen this woman before in my life.

There was only one way to get answers - by talking to a few specific people.

I got up from my chair and made my way out of my study and into my bedroom, determined to unravel this crazy mystery.

Seraphina

"I didn't expect your number to actually dial when I called it," I admitted, my eyes fixed on him.

He smiled, still recovering from the surprise of seeing me. His gaze lingered on me, and I could tell he was taken aback by how well I'd been.

I, too, was surprised to see the former basketball playboy from our school days transformed into a suit-wearing CEO before me. I felt a sense of accomplishment, knowing my hard work had paid off.

"I never changed my contact. How have you been, Sera? It's been... so long," he said, his eyes still on me, and I returned his smile.

"Well, I'm doing great. It's really nice to see you again, Sean," I replied softly.

He nodded and took a sip of his drink that had been ordered earlier. I let out a sigh.

"You mentioned you wanted to discuss something with me?" he asked.

I hesitated before diving into the question that had been weighing on my mind. "Do you still keep in touch with him?" I asked, and he immediately understood who I was referring to.

"Yes, I do. Almost all the time, and he's doing very well," he replied, his tone reassuring. I nodded, a faint smile touching my lips.

"Why do you ask?"

"I saw someone, Sean... someone who looks so much like him. Like Thad, and it's making me feel...confused. Does he live in this city?" I questioned.

Sean nodded slowly, and I pressed on with a glimmer of hope. "Is it... is it him, the one I saw? Is it Thad I saw?"

But his nod confirmed my suspicion.

"I knew this day would come, and I've secretly prepared for it. He is the one you saw, Sera. There are no two Thads in this world. He came here a few years ago to take over his dad's company. But Sera, he's a different person now, and he doesn't... remember you," Sean explained.

A mix of emotions flooded over me, but I managed to smile, tears welling up in my eyes, replacing the shock of how true it was that I had seen him.

"I haven't forgotten my promise to Vivienne. I don't plan on approaching him,"

Sean's next words took me by surprise. "Not anytime soon, but you still have to. I'm not against your relationship with him, Sera. I never have been. But I had to do what would bring peace to Thad. He was my friend. I'd love for you to meet him one day and talk to him," he said earnestly.

I nodded, looking at him and smiled, but my smile felt forced, concealing the mixture of emotions churning within me.

* * * Thad

"Thaddeus!" Mum exclaimed in shock as she watched me walk into the dining room. "You didn't tell me you would be coming, dear. I can't believe this," she added, placing the fork she held in her plate.

I let out a sigh and approached her. "I have something to ask you, Mum,"

She looked at me with those pleading grey eyes and suggested, "Why don't you join me for dinner first, and then we can discuss whatever it is you want to ask me?"

I pulled out a chair and took a seat as the maid began to serve my food.

"I'm not planning on staying for long, Mum. I'll just ask you now," I replied, starting to eat.

"Is it a question that finally brings my son to see his mother after weeks of not seeing her?" Mum asked, her lips forming a slight pout.

"Mum, we saw each other at the last charity event, remember?" I reminded her.

"That was two months ago, Thaddeus. You rarely even call me unless I do," she complained, causing me to sigh in response.

"Mum, do you remember if I ever brought a girl with chestnut brown hair home when I came home drunk during my college days, or maybe an ex I can't recall?" I inquired.

She looked surprised at my question and replied, "You brought quite a number of girls home back then, Thad. How do you expect me to keep tabs on their hair colors?"I nodded in agreement."You're right; I don't expect you to remember that. What about when I had... when I had the accident back in high school?" I asked, and her expression immediately changed.

"What about it, Thad?" she asked in a hushed tone.

"Do you know if I had a friend with chestnut hair and green eyes, maybe from my classmates or our neighbors...?" I started to inquire.But she interrupted me with a swift, "No, you didn't."

Her response was firm, and she continued, "You didn't know anyone of that description, Thad. I would have told you if you did. I've already assured you that you didn't lose memory of anyone close to you; the person is probably of no importance," she rambled on, her nervousness becoming more evident.

I couldn't ignore the anxiety in her voice and decided to press further, saying,

"Mum..."

"Why do you ask, Thad?" she interrupted me again, her tone more insistent this time.

I observed her closely, from her nervous expression to the way she absent-mindedly peeled at the skin around her nails - a telltale sign of her anxiety.

She was scared of something, that much was clear.

In an attempt to ease her worry, I gently wrapped my hands around hers and offered a reassuring smile.

"Nothing to worry about, Mum. I just saw someone who looked like that, and it felt like a déjà vu," I explained casually.

Her eyes remained desperate for any sign of my memory returning as she asked, "Are you regaining any of your past memories, Thad?You need to let me know so we can go to the doctor."

I shook my head, chuckling softly.

"No, Mum, I can't remember anything. You told me I've remembered everyone I had to, so why all the questions?"

"I am just worried," she said, giving a short laugh before turning back to her food.

We both returned to our meal, but I couldn't help but steal glances at her.

I knew she was hiding something, and while I didn't want to pressure her further, I realized that I might need to seek answers from someone else.

Chapter 6

Seraphina"I'm sorry for coming late, Senior. Luna was giving me a handful," I

apologized as I took my seat in front of him.He smiled and shook his head. "It's fine. Let's order now," he said, signaling the waiter, who promptly approached us with the menu."So, what is it that you wanted to discuss with me?" I inquired as soon as the waiter left."You won't even let me eat first, Sera?" he replied, offering a short laugh."I have an event coming up next Saturday, a charity event with a little party. I was wondering if you'd be available to go with me," he asked, his eyes fixed on me."As your date?" "Not exactly as my date, but as a companion," he clarified."Companion? That sounds like a date to me," I remarked with a playful smile."Maybe," he conceded, and I couldn't help but laugh

"Why did you deny it in the first place?" I asked, the smile on my lips widening."It's just that this is the first time I'm asking you to accompany me to an event, and..." He trailed off, a shy smile appearing on his lips.I nodded and replied, "I'll be available, Lys. I'll go with you.""Thank you, Sera," he said with gratitude in his eyes, and I smiled in response, nodding.

* * *

ThadThe intercom buzzed, and I picked it up."Yes?" "Miss Castilla is here requesting to see you," Mark's voice came through.I let out a sigh, setting aside the file I had been holding. "Let her in," I replied.A few minutes later, the door to my office swung open, and Castilla entered, carrying a basket of flowers, or rather, plants. She was dressed in her usual stylish manner."Thad," she greeted with a smile."What is this?" I asked, gesturing toward the basket she held, even though I could see the flowers peeking out - they were Peace Lilies."Flowers... for you, or rather, for your office," she replied. "I noticed that you don't have enough flowers on this side of your office, so I decided to bring them and arrange them for you.""Castilla..." I started to protest."Don't worry about me. I won't disturb your work. Just do your thing, and I'll do mine," she assured, moving to the right side of my spacious office.I couldn't help but interrupt her. "Castilla, I'm allergic to them," I admitted, and she immediately stopped, turning to look at me in shock."I'm allergic to Peace Lilies. I can't bear to have them in my office," I explained, adjusting my tie slightly.She immediately picked up the basket and walked out of my office. I let out a sigh of relief as I removed my tie completely and placed it on my desk.

I couldn't remember when this allergy had started, but I knew I'd always had it.The scent of Peace Lilies made me feel nauseous, and being exposed to them would result in me breaking out in rashes.A few minutes later, Castilla returned, her expression apologetic. "Thad, I'm

so sorry. I didn't realize you were allergic to it. No one informed me," she apologized sincerely."But you know now, so it's fine," I replied with a small smile and returned my attention to the files on my desk.Castilla shifted the topic, asking, "You still have that necklace?" and pointing to my neck."Yes," I confirmed, and she nodded in response.A moment passed, and as she prepared to leave, she reached for her bag. "I should take my leave now. Is Peace Lily the only flower you're allergic to?" she inquired, turning towards the door."Yes," She smiled slightly and nodded.

"Castilla," I called out, making her stop in her tracks and look back at me."It's your birthday on Wednesday. Let's have dinner together," I said, and a surprised smile graced her lips."I thought... you forgot," she whispe red."You're my friend, Callie. Why would I forget your birthday? I'll pick you up at 5 pm on Wednesday," I assured her."Okay. I'll be expecting you," she replied with a smile before turning and walking out of my office.* * *

SeraphinaIt had been a few days since I saw Thad, and while I missed him dearly and wished to see him again, I couldn't bring myself to break the promise I made

to Vivienne.

Eight years had passed since I last approached him, and even

though he was now in the same city as I was, I remained hesitant to reach out."Sera, the manager wants to speak with you," one of my colleagues informed me. I nodded in acknowledgment and left the bustling kitchen.I knocked on the manager's office door and entered after hearing a "come in" from her.

"You wanted to see me?" I inquired as soon as I had closed the door behind me. I was still dressed in my chef attire, complete with my cap. I couldn't

help but feel relieved that she had called me, as I had been enduring the heat of the kitchen for six straight hours.

"Yes, Sera. Please, have a seat," she responded, gesturing towards the chair in front of her desk.I let out a sigh and took a seat.

"I know this is sudden, and I'm aware you don't like this, so before you open your mouth to curse me, just hear me out," she urged, and I im- mediately knew what she was going to ask."You know our restaurant is a high-class establishment, and we have various customers who request a private chef for their romantic dates and such," she began, and I shifted in my seat, bracing myself for what was to come."I could have called Clara, but everyone knows you are still one of the best we have, Sera. A very important couple is having a dinner date here tomorrow,

and I want you to be the one to provide our services," she explained, looking at me with an apologetic expression."Sarah..." I began."I know it wasn't part of our contract, and I'm aware you don't like it, but just this once. They are VIPs at this restaurant, and I can't afford to disappoint them," she pleaded.I sighed and finally nodded. "Okay, just this once," I agreed.She smiled and expressed her gratitude. "That's why I love you, Seraphina. You're the best," she said, standing up to hug me tight.

"Careful... I have flour on my clothes," I chuckled as she held me tightly.*
* *

Thad"Thank you," Castilla said with a smile as I pulled out the chair for her to sit. I returned to my own seat, patiently awaiting the chef's arrival."I didn't know you would bring me here, Thad," she remarked, looking around the section I had rented for the night. "It's beautiful," she added."Of course it has to be. It's your birthday," I replied, earning a chuckle from her.Just as we were settling in, a voice began speaking. "Good evening, sir and ma. I will be the chef preparing your meal tonight. It's a pleasure to be here to prepare a special meal for you. My name is Chef..." The voice trailed off

as I looked up and met her gaze.Her eyes widened a bit in shock as she stared at me. I couldn't help but notice how elegant she looked in her pristine white chef attire and perfectly fitting cap, with a few strands of chestnut hair peeking out.

We locked eyes for a

moment before she cleared her throat."If you have any dietary preferences or questions about the menu, please feel free to let me know," she stammered slightly."What are you preparing for us?" Callie asked, a smile on her face."It's a secret," she replied with a small smile, and Callie chuckled in response.I couldn't help but get lost in her smile, which seemed just like the one she had when I first saw her at that event."Did you tell her not to tell me beforehand?" Callie inquired, breaking my reverie. I turned to look at her, letting out a small chuckle."No, not really," I replied, feeling my heart beat faster in my chest.Callie nodded, a smile on her face, but I could tell she wasn't entirely

convinced. I continued to watch as she began cooking, her movements precise and graceful.

Despite being entranced by her culinary expertise, my eyes kept drifting back to her face throughout the evening.She glanced up at me once and caught me staring, causing me to quickly avert my gaze, a behavior I'd never exhibited before. Slowly, I turned my head to look at her again, observing her closely, trying to recall where I might have

met her before, but my memory remained blank."Thad!" Callie's voice snapped me out of my thoughts, and I turned my head to face her."I've been calling you for a while now. You also like the way she cooks, right?" she asked, glancing over at our green-eyed chef. I nodded, adjusting my tie.

As a few minutes passed and she was engrossed in her cooking, she eventually came over to serve us, introducing the meal she had prepared. But I found myself not really listening to her words; my focus remained on her eyes,

which continued to avoid my direction."Wow, this is so lovely. Thank you," Callie exclaimed with a small clap, breaking me out of my trance.I watched as she bowed slightly and was about to leave. Without thinking, I quickly stood up, reaching out and grabbing her right wrist, causing her to stop and look at me in shock."You know me, don't you?" I asked, my words sounding uncertain."What?" she replied, her voice barely above a whis per."Do you..." I started to ask."No, I don't know you," she interrupted firmly, looking straight into my eyes and attempting to pull her hand from my grasp. I held onto it tightly."She said she doesn't know you, Thad," Callie chimed in with a short, awkward laugh.I stared into those green eyes, searching for the truth, and something inside me told me she was lying. I couldn't explain how I knew, but she definitely

knew who I was.

Slowly, I released her hand, and she turned and walked away. I watched her retreating figure before finally sitting back down."Do you know her, Thad?" Callie's voice asked, her gaze focused on me.I turned my head to look at her and let out a sigh. "No. I think I've just been under a lot of stress lately," I replied, still glancing in the direction the chef had walked off to."That's serious, Thad. You literally asked a chef you've never met before if she knows you. Don't you think you should see a doctor or..." Callie started, her concern evident."I'm fine, Callista," I interrupted her, but her worried expression persisted.I reached into my pocket and retrieved a small black box. "Here, I got this for you," I said, placing it on the table in front of her.

She gasped in surprise, and I noticed her eyes twinkling with delight as she opened the small black box and pulled out a set of earrings."You said you wanted these the last time we went to Paris," I remarked."I didn't know you noticed. Thank you so much, Thad," she replied."You're welcome," I said with a small chuckle, inwardly noting how my mom had actually mentioned the earrings to me, and I hadn't noticed it until now.* * *

SeraphinaI turned on my bed for what felt like the umpteenth time and sat up, unable to find a comfortable position to rest in. I reached for the lamp by my bedside and switched it on.Sighing, I pulled a pillow onto my chest and leaned back slightly. My thoughts raced as I whispered to myself, "I thought he lost his memory. How could he

still know that we once knew? Why did it have to be him of all people?""He's not even sure of it," I added, grappling with my conflicted emotions.Vivienne's words echoed in my head, reminding me not to approach him ever again."Stop thinking, Sera. He has a girlfriend now and is living happily. I shouldn't

ruin that for him," I told myself, making up my mind not to reveal my identity to him.Glancing at the wall clock, I saw that it was 3 a.m. I lay back down on the bed and tried to will myself to sleep, hoping to find some respite from the swirling thoughts and emotion.

ThadI groaned, my body aching as I lay sprawled on the floor. My head was resting on someone's lap, a woman dressed in a black garment.

She held me gently, her voice a

soft whisper as she gazed down at me. I struggled to focus, squinting my eyes to see her more clearly. Tears streamed down her face, her words a comforting murmur.

A sharp pain coursed through my chest, and it hurt to witness her tears. I attempted to lift my hand to wipe them away, but my limbs felt heavy, unresponsive. I strained to make out her features, but they remained blurred.

Then, she looked up at me once more, and I locked eyes with her. They were a striking shade of emerald green.PresentI shot up from my bed, gasping for breath, my heart racing as if it were trying to escape my chest.

My room was bathed in the soft morning light, and I was alone, as I always was.Sighing heavily, I climbed out of bed and checked the wall clock - it was 6 a.m. I'd had the same dream for the fourth consecutive night, a recurring vision that had haunted me since the last day I saw her."Feeling a sense of urgency and desperation, I reached for my phone on the bedside table and dialed a number, the only person who could possibly help me make sense of these unsettling dreams."Hello," came his groggy, hoarse voice on the other end."Sean," I said, my voice filled with urgency as I ran my hands through my disheveled morning hair."Oh God, man. Thad, I thought we discussed about you not calling me so early..." he began."I need help," I interjected, unable to contain my anxiety.

Chapter 7

P ast"What do you mean you're not the one? Bret claimed he saw you two in the bathroom clearly," Thad's voice boomed, his anger evident in his blazing eyes.

"Thad, when did you start giving more weight to others' words than mine? Don't you trust me?" I retorted, my patience wearing thin from the argument that had

erupted earlier in the day.

Our voices echoed through his house, making it evident

to anyone within earshot that we were locked in a heated dispute.

"I want to believe you, Sera. But what I saw is making me doubt your words," he admitted, lowering his voice.

I sighed and approached him, dressed only in my bra and underwear. "What did

you see? Huh? Show it to me," I challenged, daring him.

He retrieved his phone from the bedside table, tapped a few buttons, and then turned it towards me.

I grabbed the phone from him and played a video that was on it.

It was a video of a girl kissing a guy passionately in the school bathroom. She was moaning, and the guy had his hands wrapped around her.

One thing immediately

caught my attention - the girl in the video had hair identical to mine. The video abruptly stopped, and I looked up to find Thad's eyes fixed on me.

"You actually believed that this is me? How is that possible? I don't even moan like that, Thad!" I yelled, frustration evident in my voice.

"So you're telling me that this isn't you?" He asked, his voice seething with anger.

"Yes, it's not me, babe. How could I betray you, given everything we've been through?" I replied.

"Liar!" He yelled at my face, causing me to take a step back, fear coursing through

me.

"We've spent years together, Seraphina. We've shared countless experiences as a couple, and I've done so much for you. You can't treat me like this, Sera. You just

can't. How could you even think of being unfaithful to me? How?" He said, his voice breaking as tears welled up in his eyes.

"Thad, you really need to calm down. I'm not the one in that video," I said, taking a cautious step towards him, hoping to soothe his anger.

"So you're admitting it, Seraphina? You really did it. Don't you dare touch me," he hissed, walking away from me before I could reach out to him.

"Thad, just stop, please. I'm telling you the truth. I'm not the person in that video," I said, frustration evident in my tone.

"You keep saying the same thing, over and over. How can you open your mouth and lie to me? Uhn?" he shouted again, gripping his hair tightly in frustration.

"Thad..."

"Fuck!" He yelled, forcefully smashing his hand into a nearby mirror, causing it to shatter into pieces on the floor.

"Thad, baby, you really need to calm down. You're hurting yourself," I urged, rushing

over to him and gently taking hold of his bleeding right hand.

"Do you even love me, Seraphina? Do you love me?" He whispered, his eyes locked onto mine, searching for answers, seemingly unfazed by his injured hand.

"How can you ask me that now when your hand is bleeding, Thad?" I replied, my concern evident as I examined his injured hand closely.

"You don't. You've been deceiving me," he retorted, roughly pulling his hand away from my grasp, causing me to stumble and fall to the floor.

"Thad!" I yelled, infuriated by his actions.

"Leave me the fuck alone!" he shouted, storming off to his bathroom and slamming

the door shut behind him.

It was painful to have such an argument tonight, something that had never happened before. I couldn't tell if he was being overly protective or if he simply didn't trust me, but either way, it hurt deeply.

It stung that he wouldn't let me tend to his injury and

that the look in his eyes had changed. He had never regarded me that way before.

Tears welled up in my eyes as I slowly got up and made my way to his bed. Quietly, i picked up my clothes and started putting them on. I walked over to his wardrobe

and began packing the clothes I had brought with me for what was supposed to be a week spent together. The sense of heartache and disappointment hung heavy in the room.

As I continued packing my things, the sound of breaking and his constant screams of frustration echoed from the bathroom. It was clear that he was venting his anger, scattering everything in there.

Tears streamed down my face as I hastily grabbed my phone. I cast a hopeful glance towards the bathroom door, longing for him to step out and tell me it had all been a misunderstanding. But the door remained closed, and the silence between us seemed to grow more unbearable with every passing moment.

I walked over to his door, quietly opening it and making my way out. As I closed the door gently behind me, tears still streaming down my face, the weight of the

unresolved argument and the pain of the moment hung heavy in the air.Present"So you're telling me you saw a green-eyed lady, and you've been encountering her in your dreams lately, if I'm understanding correctly?" Sean asked, his expression marked with confusion.I sighed, feeling like I was repeating myself for the umpteenth time. "Yes,

that's it. She... she evokes these emotions in me when I see her, and she feels incredibly familiar, like someone from my past," I explained.Curiosity evident, Sean took a sip of his wine and inquired further, "What kind of emotions does she stir within you?""Weird things. I mean, not in a bad way, but she just... my heart races ten times faster than it should, and I feel overwhelmed at times. I start hearing voices in my head, and it's like I'm regaining memories from my past, Sean," I

explained, gesturing with my hands to emphasize the sensation.Sean sighed and spoke casually, "Thad, this is quite unusual for you. You're stressed." Curious, he continued, "What does she look like?"

"She's short, with a petite stature, chestnut brown hair, and green eyes. Overall, she captivates me, and I can't seem to look away when I set my eyes on her.

I've even started seeing her in my kitchen and bathroom now..."

I paused, and for a brief moment, a look of shock flashed across Sean's face before he composed himself."Maybe it's one of those girls you were involved with back in college, Thad. She might be here for some sort of revenge," he suggested, offering an

awkward chuckle as he downed his wine.I studied his face for a moment. "You do know her, don't you? You know who I'm talking about," I insisted."Me? No, I really don't. How can I remember someone I've never even seen before?" he chuckled, trying to dismiss the topic. "You should get some rest,

Thad. I'm out of this discussion," he said, rising from his seat."Where are you going? I'm not finished, Sean," I protested, watching him grab his car keys.He shook his head. "Well, I am. I can't stay here and listen to you talk about a mermaid that appears in your dreams every night. Get back to work, man,"

he said, giving my arm a playful smack. "I'm off. I've got a date with my girlfriend tonight."I sighed, feeling a sense of isolation as I watched him leave my wine room.Once he closed the door behind him, I whispered to myself, "What the hell have I gotten myself into?" The mystery of the green-eyed lady in my dreams was becoming increasingly perplexing.

Seraphina"When is Clara planning to come back? We need her here," a colleague of mine inquired, her gaze fixed on me.I grinned playfully. "Or do you just miss her?" I teased.She chuckled. "Well, you could say that," she admitted."She'll be back sooner or later," I assured her before grabbing my bag and heading for the door.

"Goodbye, see you tomorrow," I called as I closed the door behind me .Clara had been absent from work, consumed by heartbreak over Tyler, her cheating boyfriend. I had visited her house to offer comfort, but she seemed

stuck in a cycle of waking up, eating, crying, and sleeping.As I approached the back door, I realized it was closed, prompting a sigh. I retraced my steps to the main restaurant area and headed for the entrance.As I walked through the restaurant, my gaze swept around, and by chance, i locked eyes with a pair of intense grey ones-it was Thad.

A sudden rush of emotion made my heart skip a beat, and I quickly looked away, picking up

my pace as I exited the restaurant.My phone chimed with a message just as I stepped outside. It was from Lys:"I'm almost at your restaurant; I'll take you home."I smiled and was about to reply when I heard a familiar, deep voice behind me."Excuse me, excuse me!"I turned to face those striking grey eyes once more and couldn't help but notice how much Thad had changed over the eight years.

He looked more mature and handsome than I remembered from our high school days. Dressed in his signature suit, I could see his muscles straining against the fabric; Thad

had always been dedicated to his workouts.I couldn't bring myself to look directly at him and instead scanned the area around us.

"Yes?" I replied softly, my gaze still avoiding his face."Why are you avoiding me? You do recognize me, don't you?" He asked, taking a step closer. His cologne enveloped me, and I instinctively took a step

back, my heart racing."No... I... don't," I stammered, struggling to meet his gaze."You're lying, and I know it. You're avoiding my eyes," he insisted." No, I'm not," I replied, briefly glancing at his handsome face for less than two seconds before averting my gaze."If you don't know me, I certainly know you," he continued.His words left me bewildered. How could he possibly know me? Had he regained his..."I saw you at the charity event, in the elevator, at the restaurant, and now here again," he confessed earnestly. "Miss, I know I might sound strange or like a

pervert, but let me assure you, I am nothing of the sort."I knew Thad well enough to trust him. Still avoiding his eyes, I reluctantly said, "Okay," and began to turn away.

But before I could leave, he caught my wrist once more. When did this become a habit of his?"Wait, I'm not finished," he said urgently. "I need to know you."

"What?" I whispered, completely bewildered by his words."I want to know if we ever met back in college or if I've somehow offended you. But I need you to forgive me. If it's money you want, I'll give it to you, just as long as you leave me alone," he explained urgently.My confusion deepened as I finally looked directly at him. "What are you talking about?" I asked."I see you in my dreams every night, always dressed in black and crying over me. I even see you in my bathroom and kitchen sometimes. I can't seem to

get you off my mind. I'm a very busy businessman, and I can't afford to be distracted like this. Whatever it is you're doing to me, whether it's a charm, a

love potion, or a curse, you need to stop it now," he pleaded.I squinted my eyes in confusion, trying to make sense of what Thad was saying. It was clear that he had a tendency to wear his heart on his sleeve and express his feelings openly."You think I used a love potion, charm, or curse on you?" I asked, incredulous.He nodded, his expression serious.

"Yes."At his answer, I couldn't help but burst into laughter. I looked at him, and he released his grasp on my wrist, watching me curiously.

My laughter gradually

subsided, and I noticed a change in his expression-it was the same look he used to give me when we were dating, full of admiration. I immediately stopped laughing and cleared my throat."Mr...," I began."Whitlock," he whispered, his gaze fixed on me.

"Mr. Whitlock, I'll admit that I've seen you in the places you mentioned earlier, but I did not use any charm, love potion, or curse on you," I clarified,

still finding the situation somewhat amusing.His expression shifted immediately to his usual cool and composed demeanor."Then what are you? How can I dream about you consecutively for a whole week? That's ridiculous," he said, causing me to smile."It's because we keep running into each other, Mr. Whitlock. Your dreams will stop once you stop encountering me," I explained. "I have to go now," I added, turning to leave.

But he caught my hand again before I could get away."What's your name?" he inquired."Ser... Sarah. Just Sarah," I replied, correcting myself and offering a faint smile."Sarah," he repeated, then released my hand. I nodded and turned to leave, making my way to the car park.

Glancing back, I noticed he was still standing there, watching me. It seemed he couldn't take his eyes off me now either.I let out a sigh of relief as I spotted Lys's car and made my way towards it, grateful for the opportunity to leave this bewildering encounter behind me."Do you know him, Sera?" Lys asked as soon as I entered his car, his gaze fixed on Thad in the distance."Yes," I replied casually as I buckled my seat belt. Lys nodded, still keeping an eye on Thad, who remained standing and watching us.

Without further delay, Lys started the car and drove away, leaving Thad behind in our rear view mirror.

Chapter 8

I t had been a few days since I last saw Sarah, and I couldn't help but feel like a fool for believing her words. Even though we hadn't crossed paths again,

thoughts of her lingered in my mind.

In my dreams, we were holding hands, and I longed for her presence, despite knowing so little about her.

My heart raced whenever I thought about her.

A sudden knock on my office door interrupted my reverie, and I called out,

"Come in," eager to see who had come to disturb my thoughts.

Mark entered my office, his usual demeanor in place, hiding his pad the way he always did.

"I wanted to remind you about the charity event tomorrow, sir. It's a dinner party, and you'll need an escort to go with you," he informed me, glancing

briefly at his pad.

I stood up from my seat, realizing I had forgotten about the event. "I totally forgot about that. There will be no need for an escort; I'll be going alone," I replied.

Mark, however, insisted, "But sir, it's important for you to go with someone, as the event will be filled with young and old couples. So you won't feel lonely, sir," he added, subtly hinting at the potential loneliness of attending the event solo.

"Do I look lonely?" I inquired, a hint of irritation in my voice.

"No, sir. Not in any way. I was just suggesting," Mark replied, shaking his head.

I let out a sigh.

"Okay. I'll take care of it. You can go," I said, signaling for him

to leave.

He bowed slightly before exiting the room.

Alone in my office, I strolled over to the side with a view of the bustling city below. I contemplated calling Callista, not because I believed she would

refuse, but because I didn't want her to accompany me.

I could already picture

her enthusiasm if I asked her to join me at the event.

I sighed and ran my hands through my hair, finally making up my mind to call her. I retrieved my phone from my pocket and was about to dial her number when an incoming call interrupted me. It was Callista.

"Hello," I answered, my voice calm.

"Thad, I'm so sorry for calling you right now. I know you're working," she apologized, her voice soft.

"It's okay," I reassured her, stuffing my free hand into my pocket.

"I'm sure you've received an invitation to the charity event tomorrow night. I was also invited, and I know you don't have a partner, so why don't we both

go together?" Callista suggested.

I paused for a moment before replying, "Yes, we can both go there together. I'll send my driver to pick you up."

"That will be great, Thad. See you tomorrow," she replied before ending the call.

I sighed as I looked ahead, her face occupying my thoughts once again, those captivating green eyes staring at me.

"This is so messed up," I muttered under my breath, then turned and walked back to my desk, already feeling a mix of emotions about the event.

Seraphina

"How do I look?" I asked, glancing down at my attire. I wore a stylish black off-shoulder gown that flowed gracefully to the floor, featuring a subtle slit, and completed the look with matching heels.

"You look beautiful, Sera," Lys complimented, his eyes clearly captivated by my outfit. I couldn't help but smile in response.

"Shall we head out now?" he asked with a playful grin, extending his arms.

"Yes, let's go," I replied, chuckling softly as I wrapped my arms around his.

We soon arrived at the event, and it exceeded my expectations. The grand hall was filled with high-class couples and individuals, adorned with elaborate

decorations.

A scattering of bodyguards added an air of security to the scene.

Throughout the evening, I remained close to Lysander, occasionally engaging

in light conversations with other women in attendance, attempting to enjoy myself.

I strolled over to the balcony, gazing down at the cars neatly parked outside the expansive compound, their headlights casting soft glows into the night.

A warm smile graced my lips as I gazed up at the starry sky.

"Beautiful, isn't it?" I heard a voice.

Turning around, I spotted a woman dressed in a shimmering red gown, slowly

making her way toward me. I recognized her as the same girl I had seen with Thad earlier. Her eyes widened in surprise as she locked eyes with me.

"It's such a small world," she began, her voice trailing off.

"Surprising to see you here, Chef..."

"Everhart," I introduced myself with a friendly smile, and she reciprocated with one of her own.

"It's a pleasure to meet you, i am Callista," she replied, extending her hand for a handshake, which I gladly accepted.

As she sipped her wine, she inquired, "Did you come here alone? I wouldn't have expected to see you at an event like this."

"No, I'm here with a friend," I answered, and she nodded in understanding.

Returning the question, I asked, "And you? Did you come with someone?"

"I came with someone I hold dear," she replied with a cheerful laugh. "You actually saw him the other day at the restaurant."

I nodded, glancing back at the mesmerizing view before us. So, she did indeed come with him, I thought to myself.

Her phone buzzed, and she briefly answered it with a few muttered words before ending the call.

"It was lovely chatting with you, Chef Everhart, but I have a speech to deliver now," she mentioned with a warm smile.

"Likewise,"

"You seem to be a woman of few words," she noted as she walked away, and I couldn't help but smile in response.

I wasn't typically a person of few words; in fact, I tended to be quite expressive. However, the situation with Callista and Thad had left me somewhat introspective.

I whispered to myself, "Don't dwell on this, Sera. He has every right to be with the person he chooses."

As I wrapped my arms around my chest in contemplation, my gaze drifted downward, and I noticed a pool by the side of the building.

"Wow," I remarked aloud, "I didn't notice this before." I stared at the pool, momentarily lost in thought.

Swimming had never been a skill I possessed; I never learned how to swim from a young age.

Being in a pool always made me feel as though the water was overpowering me, invoking a sense of fear and helplessness.

That's why I tended to stay

away from bodies of water. Memories of swimming with Thad flooded my mind, and I couldn't help but smile, recalling how he used to playfully tease

me about my lack of swimming skills.

While I continued to peer down at the pool, my attention shifted to Lys, who emerged from the hall and strolled along a dimly lit path.

"Why is he heading in that direction? Is he looking for me?" I muttered to myself, growing curious. I quickly turned and made my way back into the hall,

increasing my pace.

Lost in thought, I accidentally bumped into someone, their shoulder colliding with mine.

A familiar cologne wafted through the air, filling my senses as I glanced up to meet a pair of surprised grey eyes.

"I'm sorry," I quickly apologized and hurriedly walked past him before he could respond. I could feel his gaze following me as I exited the hall.

Soon, I reached the path where I had seen Lysander earlier. My feet were throbbing with discomfort, so I paused and crouched down to remove my heels. As I continued walking toward the pool area, I noticed water splashed across the floor.

I sighed and halted, calling out for Lysander, "Lysander!" I repeated his name several times, but there was no response. Frustrated, I decided to return to the hall and wait for him there.

I turned and retraced a few steps back in the direction I had come from but then changed my mind and followed the path Lysander had taken.

Holding my heels in one hand and lifting my gown with the other, I navigated cautiously over the slippery floor.

"I'm getting tired of all this. I can't wait to leave," I quietly muttered to myself as I moved forward, my frustration growing.

Suddenly, I heard my name being called, "Chef Everhart."

I looked up to see who it was, though I already had a feeling about the caller's identity. Just as I did, my foot slipped, causing me to fall backward right into the pool beside me.

I could see the shock on Callista's face as she peered down from the balcony where she stood.

* * *

Thad

I chuckled at a witty remark made by one of my business partners,

continuing to sip the wine in my hand.

However, I couldn't shake the image of her face from my mind. She had appeared so stunning and delicate, even if it was just for a brief moment.

Thoughts swirled in my head. Who had she come to the event with? Did she have a boyfriend or was she married? These questions made me unconsciously

clench my jaw as I gently placed the wine glass on the table. I made up my mind to leave the gathering, ready to leave.

I noticed Callista approaching me with a terrified look in her eyes, her fear evident as she moved closer.

"Callie," I said as soon as she reached me.

She breathed out in distress and spoke with a voice trembling like a scared kitten, "She fell into the pool."

Confusion washed over me as I asked, holding both of her hands to soothe her, "Who are you talking about?"

"The...chef. The chef we met the last time we went to the restaurant on my birthday," she stammered. It took me a moment to fully grasp what she had just said.

I swiftly pulled my arm from her grasp and moved past her, determined to take action.

"Where are you going?" Callista asked, her voice filled with worry.

"To save her," I replied without hesitation.

But she was resolute. "No," she insisted firmly, "let someone else do it, please. What if something happens to you? We can call security to handle it. You can't even swim," she reminded me.

"Who told you I can't swim?" I shot back, frustration in my voice as I roughly freed my hand from her grasp and sprinted towards the door leading to the pool area.

As I hurried down the stairs and approached the door leading to the pool area, one thought echoed in my mind, a stark realization: She couldn't swim.

She had no idea how to swim.

Chapter 9

Past"I won't hurt you, I promise," Thad reassured me, gently holding my waist as he tried to coax me into the water.

We were in the backyard of his house, him sporting swimming shorts while I sat at the edge in my brand new swimsuit and undies.

"No, I'm scared," I protested, resisting his gentle pull by clutching onto his hands.

This had become a recurring argument between us.

"What if you lose your grip on me? I could drown, Thad," I whined.

"I won't. Don't you trust me?" he said, laughing.

"I do. But don't make fun of me," I complained, playfully smacking his arms. His response was a groan of mock pain.

"I'm not making fun of you, but that really hurts," Thad complained, pouting in mock pain.

"But you're laughing," I pointed out, gesturing to his grinning face.

"I am not," he protested before succumbing to another fit of laughter.

"Alright, babe, I'm sorry. Just swim with me this once," he pleaded, his hands still securely around my waist.

"No," I replied, shaking my head stubbornly.

"I'll pull you in, Sera," he threatened.

"No, you won't," I challenged.

"I will," he declared, and with that, he yanked me into the water by my waist. I let out a startled scream, quickly wrapping my arms around his neck as he swam us to the center of the pool, a mischievous smile on his face.

"See, nothing happened. I don't know why you're so scared of a pool, Seraphina," Thad remarked as we floated in the water.

I couldn't help but pout, burying my face into his neck.PresentMemories of Thad flooded my mind, and I felt myself sinking deeper into the pool of nostalgia. The ache of missing him was almost unbearable, especially when we kept crossing paths and I had to pretend I didn't know

him.

The longing for his touch and his kisses was overwhelming, but I felt as helpless as I did eight years ago. As my eyelids drooped, I saw a figure lean into the pool, swiftly swimming towards me. who could it be?ThadI groaned with effort as I pulled her out of the water, laying her down carefully by the side of the pool."Sarah, Sarah. Can you hear me? Open your eyes, please," I pleaded, lightly tapping her cheek. There was no response from her.Without wasting a moment, I began performing CPR, feeling the softnessbof her lips against mine. It wasn't perfect, but I knew I had to try.

I stopped compressions, looking down at her pale, wet face and the hair spread out on the ground. She looked so fragile and vulnerable.I held her close to my chest, anxiously repeating, "Sarah, can you hear me? Please, open your eyes."After a tense moment, I heard her cough, and I quickly moved her away from my chest. She spat out some water, trying to catch her breath.

I gently rubbed her back to help her calm down."Sera, Sera!" A voice called out, and we both turned to see a blonde-haired guy rushing toward us. I slowly withdrew my hand from her back, allowing

him to crouch down beside her."Oh, thank God, you're safe," the blonde-haired guy said, gripping Sarah's shoulders tightly. "I'll take it from here," he added, briefly glancing at me.But why did he call her "Sera"?

Confusion gnawed at me.

"Can you walk?" he asked Sarah, who nodded faintly. He helped her to her feet, but she stumbled and nearly fell.

In a flash, he scooped her up in a bridal carry, cradling her in his arms.I couldn't explain why, but watching them like that ignited a sudden, un-explained rage within me.I sat there, seething with a mix of anger and frustration as I watched him carry her away. It felt unjust to me, even though it was clear that she had come with him.

"What the hell is wrong with me?" I muttered under my breath, still seated on the floor.Then, a rush of memories flooded my mind. I recalled a mo-ment in the past, swimming in a pool with a girl, holding her waist tightly as she clung onto me.

The memory was painful, and I groaned, clutching my head. I attempted to stand up, but a sudden weakness overcame me, causing me to collapse back onto the floor in agony."See, nothing happened. I don't know why you're so scared of a pool, Seraphina," I heard my own voice echoing in my head, the words vibrating in my memory.When the girl in the memory looked up, it was those green eyes that gazed at me with affection.The pain in my head ceased, and I slowly opened my eyes. Tears welled up as I realized that I had remembered this particular memory with clarity."Her name is not Sarah. It is Sera, Seraphina," I whispered to myself, my gaze fixed on the direction they had gone.Even though my memories of her were still fragmented, I had a deep sense that she was someone of great significance to me. It felt as if she was a missing half of myself, and I could sense the importance of our connection.

I had never experienced such panic for someone falling into a pool as I did for her.My heart had raced when I pulled her out earlier. Seraphina was more than just a casual friend; she held a special place in my life, even if I couldn't yet remember the details."Thad!" I heard my name, and my head snapped up to see Callista rushing toward me, with my assistant Mark close behind.She crouched down beside me, gripping my hands tightly as she examined my condition. Concern radiated from her face and voice as she asked, "Are you okay? Huh?"I looked into her eyes, which were hazel, just as they had always been. But there was no sparkle in them, unlike the green ones I had just seen in my memory of Seraphina."Answer me," she pleaded, and I mustered a slow nod before my eyelids grew heavy, and I collapsed into her arms.Suddenly, I felt my strength drain away, and my world plunged into

darkness. It was as if a truck had run over my body, and my eyes struggled to stay open.When I finally managed to open them again, I found myself in a dimly lit room.I was weak, and every part of my body ached. To my left, I saw someone holding my hand and bowing their head beside me. It was Callista.

How had she managed to bring me home?My eyelids closed again, despite my reluctance to surrender to sleep.I detected movement beside me, signaling that Callista must have awoken."You make me worry easily, Thad, and I feel like I'll grow old quickly when it comes to your matters," she whispered, her fingers still gently clasping mine.I was puzzled by her words, wondering what she meant by growing old quickly in relation to me.What is she talking about?As I lay there with my eyes closed, I sensed her rising from beside me. Before I could react, I felt her soft lips pressing against mine, her kiss gentle and fleeting.

"I like you, I always have, so please wake up" she whispered, her words hanging in the air. Then, she left the room.Her confession left me bewildered. Since when had she felt this way, and how had I never noticed? My thoughts swirled in my mind as I settled back into bed and drifted back to sleep.Seraphina

I slowly opened my eyes as the morning light shone through my curtains, floods of memories of last night came to me.I remembered how his voice was begging me to open my eyes and I have heard it from a far distance. I also remembered how his cologne filled my nose the moment I flickered my eyes open in his arms, it felt pleasing even

though it was for a brief moment making me to crave for him more.I shook my head a little as I sat up, reminding myself to stay away from him. I made my way slowly to the bathroom to do my usual morning routine and dressed up.My phone buzzed and I picked it up from the bed."Hello" "Sera, how are you feeling? I bought some drugs for you last night and place it in your living room, I am not sure if you saw them" Lys voice broke

through.I made my way to the living room still clutching my phone and saw a little white nylon filled with drugs on my couch."Thank you Lys, I just saw it now"I said, grabbing the nylon."How do you feel now? Don't you think we should go to the hospital?" He asked."There is no need for that Lys, you already asked me last night and I am sorry for troubling last night. The seat of your car must be wet now" I said, feeling down for sitting in his car with my wet cloth.

"Who cares about that Sera? You almost died last night" he said."Oh right Senior. How did you know that I was in the pool?" I asked." I was looking for you and overheard some security saying that a girl fell into the pool. I came there and found out that you were the one" he said making me to nod."Okay""Is there something wrong?" He asked."No""The guy that pulled you out, was the guy I saw at your restaurant right?""Yes. He is just...""Someone you know" he completed my sentence making me to give a short laugh."I have to go now Lys." I said and we bade bye before cutting the call.I made my way out of the house to my car and typed in Clara's location in my map. I need to talk some sense into that girl.Thad"Why did you lie to me?" I repeated, my voice growing louder. I had been talking with Sean for over 30 minutes, and he seemed unwilling to admit that

he knew Seraphina.

We sat on the balcony of my house."What the hell are you talking about, man?" Sean responded, still chuckling."It's her. Seraphina. Her name is Seraphina. Why didn't you tell me?" I demanded, and Sean's expression shifted."How did you..." he began, but I interrupted him."Who is she, Sean? She's making me feel things I haven't felt in a long time. You need to tell me now," I insisted, locking eyes with him."You'll have to find that out yourself. I'm not in any position to tell you," Sean replied, avoiding my gaze and looking down.I grew increasingly frustrated. "Are you serious right now? We've been friends for years, Sean. What kind of friends are we if you can't share things like this with me? My memory of her is still fragmented," I yelled, rising from my chair."What's going to change if you remember her completely, huh?" Sean yelled, rising abruptly from his chair. "You don't have the right to remember her now if you couldn't remember her back then. Why are you trying to do what

you should have done a long time ago? As if it's going to change anything," he continued.I took a deep breath, trying to calm myself. "So you do know who she is. Why did you lie to me at first? What happened back then, Sean?" I asked, my voice softer now.Sean sighed and ran his hands through his hair in frustration."Because of you. I'm doing this to protect you, Thad.

But if you really want to delve deep and find out what really happened, you're free to do so. Go as deep as you want. I'm giving you my support. But don't expect me to tell

you anything about her, because I won't. You should find out for yourself," he explained before grabbing his phone from the table and making his way out."Fuck!" I yelled, slamming my hands down in frustration.

Chapter 10

Seraphina"How did you turn into this, Clara?" I complained for what felt like the umpteenth time as I wiped a stain of golden morn off the floor. She remained seated on the couch, curled up in it."I know you loved Tyler a lot, but this isn't right. You're becoming miserable because of him, and I'm here working and cleaning..." I continued.Suddenly, she abruptly stood up, causing me to fall back in fear with a startled scream. I looked up at her in shock, taken aback by her sudden action."What's wrong?" I whispered, searching her face for answers."I've made up my mind, Sera," she replied, her face now swollen. I leaned in, curious."To do what?" I asked."I'm going to beat him up," she declared, looking down at me. "I'm going to beat Tyler up."I scoffed and dropped the cloth I was using to clean the floor, taken aback by her unexpected words.

ThadI parked my car in the restaurant's parking lot and made my way toward the entrance."Hi," I greeted, and the lady behind the counter looked up at me.

Her expression turned to one of admiration as she stared at my face. I cleared my throat, and she quickly snapped out of it."How may I help you, sir?" she asked in a professional tone."I'm here to see Seraphina," I stated."Sera? You mean Chef Sera?" she inquired.I nodded in confirm ation."Give me a minute, sir," the lady behind the counter said before turning to whisper to a guy nearby who promptly left his post."She should be here anytime now. Why don't you take a seat and wait for her, sir?" she suggested."Okay, thank you," I replied, following her suggestion and taking a seat at a table.After a few minutes, I saw Seraphina come out and approach the girl who had pointed at me. As she glanced in my direction, I could see the shock on

her face.

She started walking toward me, and I couldn't help but notice that

she wasn't in her chef attire. She looked stunning in her outfit, and I found it difficult to take my eyes off her."What are you doing here?" Seraphina asked as she took a seat in front of me."Is that the first thing you'd say to someone who saved your life a few nights ago?" I replied with a hint of amusement.She sighed. "Thank you for saving me that night," she said. "So why do you want to see me, Mr. Whitlock?"

I raised an eyebrow. "Why do you keep calling me that?""What?" she asked, clearly puzzled."Mr. Whitlock. Why do you keep using my surname when you know my name?" I questioned."I don't think we're that close for me to call you by your name""Oh, really? Then why did you lie to me?" I asked, leaning in closer and resting my arms on the table. My proximity seemed to catch her off guard."What..." she stammered."You lied to me about your name. Why did you do that?" I inquired, my voice low and hoarse."Stop," she said, leaning back in her chair to distance herself from me."What?" "Whatever you're trying to do with your voice, just stop it," she insisted before abruptly standing up. "I'm leaving," she declared and began walking out of the restaurant.I swiftly stood up and followed her outside, determined to catch up."Why? Am I making you feel things you haven't felt in a long time?" I yelled as I trailed behind her.She continued walking without responding.

"That's how you're making me feel," I continued, my words pouring ou t."Especially during the day and now. I see you everywhere, can't get you out of my mind, and I dream about you all the time. My memory is a mess, and, you

know what? I think I might actually like you, even though I don't know much about you. At the party the other day, somehow I just knew you couldn't

swim, and I was panicking, and-"I abruptly stopped when she suddenly came to a halt.She turned to look at me, her expression inquisitive. "How did you know that I was in the pool?" she asked.I took a few steps closer to her and gazed down at her. "Is that what you're asking after everything I've been rambling about?" I responded."Just answer the question," she insisted.I sighed. "Someone told me," I admitted.She didn't respond and turned away, continuing to walk."Seraphina!" I yelled, causing her to stop abruptly."Why did you lie about your name? Your name is Seraphina, not Sarah," I said, lowering my voice.She slowly turned and approached me, tears glistening in her eyes."Did you ask around for my name?" she inquired."Why would I do that? I remembered it. How? By regaining a memory of you

clinging to me in the pool," I replied, my frustration evident."What do you want from me?" she asked, her eyes shimmering.

"You," I answered honestly. "I want to know more about you and what happened years ago. My memory of you is distorted right now, and I need you to help me make things clear, Sera," I pleaded."It's too late. Nothing will change even if you remember me. Let's just leave it as it is," Seraphina said, turning to go. But I swiftly grabbed her hand."Nothing will change?" I questioned. "You're making me feel things, Sera. Crazy things I can't even fathom. How do you expect me to just leave it like this?" I pleaded."What exactly am I making you feel?" she yelled."Love," I admitted. "I like you so much, even though I feel like you're both close and distant. I'm craving your touch, and sometimes I feel like kissing

the hell out of you," I muttered, briefly glancing at her lips.She gazed at me for a moment, her expression a mixture of shock and sadness, before slowly shaking her head and pulling her hand away from my grasp."You shouldn't feel this way towards me. It's dangerous for you. You should stay away from me," she warned, tears streaming down her cheek."Sera, what's wrong?" I asked, taking a step closer to her in concern."Stay away from me. Don't come near me!" she suddenly yelled, taking a step back from me. "This is what I feared the most, and I prayed it wouldn't come

true.

I don't want you to become like this because of me," she whispered."What are you talking about?" I called out, but she had already turned and began walking away before I could finish.I attempted to walk after her, but a sudden ringing in my head overwhelmed me, causing me to clutch my head and groan in pain."What you call love is an obsession, Thaddeus. You're obsessed with her!" a voice screamed in my head, making me fall to my knees while still holding my head.I saw Sera stop and turn back toward me, her eyes widening in shock as she witnessed my state.

Without hesitation, she began running in my direction.

I fell to the ground, feeling utterly weak as the ringing in my ears persi sted."Thad! Thad! Please, don't do this to me. I'm sorry for yelling, I'm sorry," she pleaded, her voice filled with anguish, as she crouched down, tears streaming

down her face.

She pulled me into her arms, embracing my head, and I could

see panic and fear in her eyes.Suddenly, I experienced a deja vu at that moment, as if this same scenario had happened before. She was calling my name and crying, just like the way she

did in my dream.

I watched her gaze down at me, tears falling, as darkness

gradually enveloped me.

Chapter 11

P^{ast}

I stepped out of the taxi and once again rejected Thad's call, which had been coming in repeatedly since I left his house just a few minutes ago.

I sighed as I entered my house and slammed the door shut behind me.

"Sera, what's wrong? I thought you said you were spending the night at Thad's place," my mum said, emerging from the kitchen.

"Well, I'm not. Not anymore," I replied, making my way upstairs with my bag.

"What happened?" she asked, clearly surprised.

"We fought. He accused me of cheating, Mum, and showed me some silly video of a girl in a bathroom," I explained, tears welling up in my eyes once more.

"What do you mean? Why would you cheat on Thad?" she asked.

"I didn't, Mum. I didn't do it. I could never cheat on him. I love him so much," I protested, my voice breaking as tears streamed down my cheeks.

She sighed and pulled me into a comforting embrace. "It's okay, sweetheart. Don't cry. You need to calm down," she reassured me.

My phone buzzed again, and Thad's name lit up on my screen.

"He's been calling me, Mum, but I don't want to talk to him, not after what he said to me," I told her, pulling away from her comforting embrace.

"You should pick up his call or go back to him, okay? You know Thad won't sleep if you're not beside him," Mum urged.

"He should try to put up with me not being by his side tonight," I retorted.

"You can't do that to him, Sera. He's probably on his way here right now. Go back to him now, and I'll bring your bags there tomorrow, okay?" Mum suggested, rubbing my back gently.

I nodded and started making my way out of the house. "Goodnight, Mum," I said as I closed the door behind me and left our compound.

I stepped outside and tried to hail a taxi, but there was none in sight. After a few minutes of standing and rejecting multiple calls from Thad, I started walking down the street, hoping to find a taxi. It was 9 pm, and it was getting late.

His call came in again, and I sighed. Just as I was about to answer it, the call suddenly cut off. I sighed once more in frustration and continued walking down the street.

"Why are there no taxis for crying out loud?" I muttered under my breath.

A few minutes into my walk, I noticed a group of people gathered not too far away.

They were pointing at something and whispering. Intrigued, I followed their gaze and saw a red car, flipped upside down, with one side severely damaged.

It wasnevident that a serious accident had occurred, and I recognized the car immediately; it belonged to Thad.

"No... no... no," I muttered in shock as I started running towards the scene with all my might. Two men had approached the car and yanked the door open.

They carefully pulled Thad out and laid him on the ground.

I rushed over to them and crouched down beside Thad, pulling him onto my lap as one of the men called for an ambulance.

Thad's face was covered in blood, and there were several cuts and scrapes on his body. His eyes were closed, and blood oozed from a wound on his head.

Shards of glass were scattered around him.

"Thad! Thad! Thaddeus, please open your eyes. Don't do this to me. I'm sorry, I should have picked up your call. I'm so sorry. Please, wake up!" I cried out, sobbing uncontrollably into the night, more than I had ever cried before.

His eyes slowly fluttered open a little, and he looked up at me.

"Sera," he croaked out weakly.

"Yes, it's me. I'm so sorry, please don't leave me," I sobbed, holding Thad close to my chest.

"The ambulance will be here any minute now," the man who had called for help said, but I didn't acknowledge him or respond.

My entire focus was on Thad, who was barely conscious in my arms.

"Don't leave me alone," Thad whispered, struggling to catch his breath.

"I won't, I promise. I have no intention of leaving you, so please, stay awake. Please," I pleaded, shaking my head as tears streamed down my face.

Thad groaned in pain, and his eyes slowly closed, causing me to scream out in agony.

Present

The doctor reassured me, saying, "It's a minor fainting episode likely due to stress. He should wake up soon." I nodded, relieved to hear the doctor's assessment.

"Thank you so much, doctor," I expressed my gratitude as he left the ward with a few nurses.

I returned to Thad's bedside, taking a seat next to him. Gazing at his face, I couldn't help but notice how much he had grown since our high school days.

His jawline was chiseled, and his eyelashes seemed longer. I found my eyes drifting down to his lips, and an intense desire welled up within me to feel them against mine.

I couldn't resist the temptation as I leaned in closer to Thad's face. My hands trembled as they trailed gently against his features, but I quickly pulled back, scolding myself for getting lost in the moment.

"Get a grip, Sera," I muttered to myself, directing my attention to my own hands. However, my focus was abruptly interrupted by a groan from Thad.

I glanced up and saw that his eyes were open. In a rush, I stood up and hovered over him.

"Thad! Can you hear me? Are you okay?" I asked, my voice filled with concern.

Helping him sit up, I waited anxiously for his response

He continued to look at me, his eyes filled with amusement.

"Don't tell me you don't remember what happened? Uhn? How many fingers is this?" I asked, holding up two fingers in front of his face. "Does your head hurt? Are you in pain?" I inquired, my concern evident as I gently touched his face and ran my fingers through his soft black hair. Thad chuckled, a sound that both irritated and intrigued me. "I didn't know you cared this much about me," he remarked, and I hastily withdrew my hands from his face.

"What?"

He gave a short, amused laugh.

"I think you do, very much because if not, you wouldn't have been crying over me back at the restaurant, begging me to open my eyes," he said, his grey eyes fixed on me.

"I did that because I was scared that something happened to you," I replied, my voice softer now, my concern evident.

"Something did happen to me. Up here," he said, pointing at his head.

"Your head? Then let's tell the doctor," I suggested, turning towards the door.

"No, you don't have to do that. I'm fine now," he assured me, stopping me in my tracks.

I sighed and felt my cheeks warm up.

"Okay," I whispered, still avoiding his gaze. The room was filled with an awkward silence, and I could sense his eyes on me.

"Why are you looking at me that way?" I finally asked, feeling self-conscious.

"Because you're beautiful," he replied, his words catching me by surprise.

I chuckled softly. "You must have a thing for saying that same sentence to me," I remarked, recalling how he had said it to me multiple times in the past.

"That means you must have heard it from me before, in the past," he said, his words hinting at something more.

"It doesn't matter anymore,I am taking my leave now" I softly uttered, my voice carrying a touch of resignation.

With a slow, deliberate pace, I approached his bedside, my steps echoing in the room. My fingers brushed against the chair as I retrieved my handbag.

Unexpectedly, he reached out, his fingers gently encircling my waist, pulling me close. A rush of surprise swept through me, causing me to stumble and fall onto his chest. Our eyes locked in a moment of unspoken tension, emotions swirling in the air between us.

"Well, it does to me, everything about you matters to me. " his voice was a gentle whisper, brushing against my face like a soft breeze.

My eyes drifted down to his lips, a magnetic pull I couldn't resist. In the past, I might have leaned in for a kiss, but now, courage eluded me.

"I suppose I'm not the only one," he continued in a husky tone, his words laden with vulnerability.

"The way you affect me, Seraphina, I can't help but think I'm affecting you too." The unspoken emotions in the room hung heavy, like a question that begged to be answered.

"What are you doing?" I asked, my voice barely above a whisper, my tone filled with caution.

"I'm looking into your eyes," he replied softly. "They have this way of drawing me in every time I see them." A gentle flutter stirred in my stomach at his words.

"I must have said that before too," he murmured.

"I don't recall you saying that before," I retorted, my voice firm now. "Now, please, get your hands off me." I attempted to pull away from his grasp, but he held me firmly against his chest, refusing to let go. "You're lying," he whispered against my ear, his warm breath sending shivers down my spine. "I'll only release you when you say the truth."

With a reluctant sigh, I relented, my voice softening. "Alright, fine. You've said it to me multiple times, and I've grown tired of hearing it from you," I admitted, my words laced with a hint of exasperation. A smile played upon his lips, and suddenly, he released his hold, allowing me to slide off his chest. I straightened my clothing and let out a relieved sigh, the tension in the room dissipating.

"Thad!" A voice called from the doorway, and we both turned our heads.

Callista entered and hurriedly moved toward Thad, wrapping her arms around him in an embrace that caught him off guard. "God, you scared me," Callista said, her concern evident.

A sudden pang of hurt and jealousy welled up within me, even though I knew it made no sense. After all, I had been the one in his arms moments ago, yet now it felt like another woman had claimed what used to be mine.Thad noticed the expression on my face and reacted swiftly, gently pulling Callista away. "I'm okay, Callie, you can let go now," he assured her.

My unease deepened as I realized he had a nickname for her. "Are you sure you're okay? Does your head hurt?" Callista asked, her concern palpable as she reached for his head.

Thad, however, intercepted her hand.

"I'm fine," he insisted, making an attempt to rise from his seated position. "I need to go now."

"You can't leave yet. We still need to talk to the doctor and find out more about what's happening to you," she protested, her tone filled with worry.

The tension in the room seemed to grow as I watched the interaction between them, feeling like an outsider.I cleared my throat, drawing their attention away from their conversation.

"I'll take my leave now," I announced, my voice steady.

Callista got up and approached me. "You should Chef Everhart, thank you for helping him," she said, and I nodded.

As I started to make my way towards the door, Callista turned her attention to me once more.

"How have you been since the other night? I'm really sorry I didn't ask when I first came in," she inquired with genuine concern.

"I'm doing fine," I replied, offering a small smile. With each step closer to the door, I could feel Thad's gaze on me, a silent plea for me to stay that tugged at my heart.

Chapter 12

Seraphina

"I get that they're friends, but does she have to hug him like that? Right in front of me?" I scoffed, taking a bite of stir fry as I glanced over at Luna, my furry companion.

"Isn't that right, Luna? He's always been mine from the very beginning," I continued, speaking slowly as if trying to convince myself. I reached for a can of beer and took a sip, the liquid offering a temporary solace.

I found myself talking to myself, confessing my feelings for Thad, even though he wasn't there in my house with me.

Eventually, exhaustion overtook me, and I slipped into a deep slumber, still entangled in thoughts of him.

My room was cast in a dim, muted light as I lay asleep on my bed. A sudden sensation of soft, firm hands gliding up my thighs and under my shorts made me gasp softly.

Turning to my side, I was met with the sight of Thad, his eyes filled with admiration.

"Thad, what are you doing here? How did you—" I began, but he hushed me with a gentle shush, leaning closer.

His lips met mine in a tender, unhurried kiss, sending a shiver down my spine.

I moaned softly against his lips, feeling his hands moving beneath my shorts. He withdrew slightly, gazing down at me with desire in his eyes.

I couldn't resist; I grasped his face and kissed him again, my heart racing as his hands continued their tantalizing movements.

However, a buzzing phone suddenly pierced the moment, causing me to pull away, my thoughts jolted back to reality.

I shot up in bed, gasping, and quickly reached for my buzzing phone alarm.

As I silenced it, I glanced to my side, only to find an empty space next to me.

Reality settled in, and I realized with a gasp that I had just had a vivid and racy dream about Thad.

I couldn't help but groan, bringing my hands to my face in embarrassment.

"Why on earth did I have such a silly dream about him?" I muttered to myself, releasing my grip on my face.

"Is it because I was thinking about him all through last night?" I pondered aloud, my thoughts wandering as I tried to make sense of the unexpected dream.

"Oh no, Sera," I groaned, falling back onto the bed, my frustration and disappointment with myself evident.

The dream had left me feeling confused and flustered, and I couldn't help but wish I could erase it from my mind.

Thad

I glanced at my wristwatch for what felt like the umpteenth time, silently hoping that the seemingly endless meeting would come to an end soon.

The man at the front of the room finally concluded his presentation, bringing the slides to a halt.

I nodded, eager to make my exit, and stood up abruptly from my chair, causing the heads of the board of directors to turn their attention toward me.

I was just about to turn and leave when Mark's voice caught me off guard.

"Sir," he began, making me turn to face him.

"Yes?"

"You haven't provided a review of his presentation," he reminded me, a realization dawning on me that I had nearly overlooked this task.

"Oh... uhm. That was an excellent presentation," I managed to say, casting a brief glance at the presenter.

Without further delay, I hurriedly left the room, with Mark trailing behind me, clearly puzzled by my abrupt departure.

Once we reached my office, Mark inquired, "Do you have an appointment, Mr. Whitlock?"

"Yes, I do," I replied, my thoughts consumed by a mental image of her face.

"I'm leaving now. Please send me an email with the rest of my tasks for the day. I'll handle them tonight." I grabbed my car keys and jacket, determined to keep my appointment with her.

"Okay, sir," Mark replied, still clearly surprised by my unexpected actions.

I wasted no time and swiftly made my way out of my office.

Seraphina

"I really don't know what's wrong with you, Sera. Are you pregnant or something?" Clara asked, her irritation evident as my sighing had been quite frequent lately.

"Clara," I called her attention.

"What?" she responded, a bit exasperated.

"Is it normal to have a bad dream about someone you once loved and still love?" I asked, gazing at her with uncertainty.

"You mean your boyfriend?" she inquired.

"No, I mean... not anymore," I replied, my voice tinged with a hint of sadness.

"It depends on the kind of dream," Clara said thoughtfully. "How bad is it? Death? Sickness?" She probed, trying to understand the nature of my dream.

"It's a racy dream," I whispered, and Clara gasped.

"You had a racy dream about the blue-eyed guy?" she asked, her eyes widening.

"No, not him. It's someone else," I clarified.

"Someone else? Have I been staying at your house crying over Tyler for that long without knowing you're seeing someone else?" she exclaimed, a mix of surprise and concern in her voice.

"Okay, okay. What kind of racy dream is it then?" she inquired, her curiosity piqued.

"I can't say it," I replied, shaking my head slightly.

"Is it that bad?" Clara asked, her brows furrowing in concern, to which I nodded in confirmation.

She suddenly smiled and playfully smacked my arm.

"What was that for?" I asked, holding my arm in mock pain.

"I'm happy for you, girl. Your sexual motivation is coming back after years of its absence," she said with a mischievous grin, making me roll my eyes in disgust.

"So who is the guy, huh? Who is he?" she prodded, playfully tugging at my arm.

"I'm not discussing this. I'm leaving," I declared, freeing myself from her hold and grabbing my bag.

"Sera, wait!" she called out, but I didn't pay heed as I made my way through the restaurant toward the exit.

I stepped outside and found the rain falling heavily. Letting out a sigh, I held my handbag over my head, preparing to dash through the rain when a shadow suddenly cast over me.

I looked up and met those familiar gray eyes, belonging to Thad, who was holding an umbrella over my head.

"Thad?" I breathed out, taken aback by his unexpected presence. Memories of my recent dream with him flooded my thoughts, and I felt my cheeks flush as I looked at his lips.

"Let's go. I'll drop you off at your house," he offered.

"No, you don't have to do that. I can just take a taxi," I protested, my hands shaking slightly.

"I'll put the umbrella away soon," he replied, and I reluctantly walked alongside him, sheltered under the umbrella.

Suddenly, he wrapped his arms around my waist, pulling me closer to him, leaving me flustered and speechless.

"Get closer or you'll get wet," Thad urged, and I nodded shyly, feeling the electric charge in the air that made me unconsciously bite my lip.

As we sat in his car, I looked at him, realizing his vehicle had broken down during our journey, and he had attempted to fix it but couldn't figure out the issue.

"What should we do now?" I inquired, uncertainty creeping into my voice.

His clothes clung to his body, still damp from the rain, and he let out a sigh of frustration as he dialed his car engineer's number once more.

"My house is just down the street," I offered, my voice hesitant. I didn't really want to invite him over, but I felt compelled to help.

He pondered for a moment, and I quickly reassured him, "Don't worry, I don't plan to do anything bad to you," wanting to make my intentions clear.

A smirk played on his lips as he looked at me, his voice husky as he responded, "I should be the one saying that, Sera," sending my heart into a wild rhythm.

***

"Take these, you can shower in the guest room and change. I'll make us some tea," I said, handing him a pair of male clothes.

He looked at the clothes curiously and asked, "How do you have these? Do they belong to your boyfriend?"

I let out a sigh. "No, they belong to some of my male colleagues who occasionally sleep over after group dinners, so they keep a spare set just in case," I explained.

He nodded and accepted the clothes, eyeing me suspiciously before heading into the guest room.

I took the opportunity to go to my own room, where I quickly shed my clothes and took a refreshing shower.

A few minutes later, I emerged from the bathroom, dressed in a loose t-shirt and shorts, my hair pulled up into a bun.

I started making tea in the kitchen when I heard his voice behind me. I turned to look at him, my gaze involuntarily trailing over his body in the clothes. They fit him perfectly, accentuating his muscled arms, and I couldn't help but gulp nervously.

"How did you get this?" he inquired, holding up a picture. I looked closer and realized it was a picture of the two of us at a beach we had visited together.

I tried to grab the picture from him, but he raised his hand, preventing me from taking it. He insisted, "No... no. You don't get to take it until you answer my question," his gaze fixed on me.

I let out a sigh and took a step back. "We both took it... together," I replied, hoping to leave it at that.

But he pressed further, asking, "Is that all? No reason for us taking it together?"

"We, uh... we went to the beach together with some friends, and one of them took the picture," I explained, hoping he wouldn't dig deeper.

However, he surprised me by asking, "Why?"

"What?" I stammered.

"Why did we both go to the beach together?" he questioned. I closed the distance between us, standing on my tiptoes to meet his height, feeling the tension in the air.

"Do you want to know why?" I replied in a voice barely above a whisper, locking my gaze with his. He seemed entranced, and I could see it in his eyes.

"Yes," he said, his gaze fixed on my lips. Seizing the opportunity, I swiftly grabbed the picture from his hand and took a step back, laughing.

"Learn not to let your guard down, Thad. You'll have to figure out the story behind that picture on your own," I teased, a smile on my face.

He chuckled. "You got me there, Sera."

"I knew it would always work on you," I quipped as I returned to the kitchen counter.

"You what?" he asked, puzzled.

"Nothing," I said, sliding the picture into the pocket of my shorts.

I reached for the kettle, intending to lift it, but it was scalding hot. I dropped it to the floor immediately, the boiling water spilling across the tiles, and I clutched my burned hand against my chest in pain.

"Sera," Thad called out, rushing toward me.

"I'm fine, I'm fine. Be careful of the water," I reassured him, my eyes focused on the spilled water, but he seemed determined to help. He grabbed my hands and gently pulled me toward the sink, turning on the tap.

"It's just a little…" I started to say, attempting to pull my hand away, but his grip on my wrist tightened, and he looked up at me with a determined expression.

"Just stay still, Seraphina," he muttered, turning his attention back to my hand.

He carefully wiped away the spilled hot water and then guided me to the end of the counter.

With his arm wrapped around my waist, he effortlessly lifted me and placed me on the counter.

Stay here," he instructed, and then he began cleaning up the water on the floor. "I'll make the tea myself too"

I nodded, watching him silently.

Unbeknownst to him, tears welled up in my eyes. I hadn't realized just how much I had missed him until now. As I saw him cleaning up and taking care of me, I couldn't help but wish that he never had to leave me again.

***I didn't know you could make such good tea. Your tea always had too much water before," I whispered as I sipped the tea.

We were seated in my living room, watching a movie he had chosen, and it felt strangely like a date. "I've learned a few things over the years," he replied with a smile, and I nodded in acknowledgment. "So, are you ready to tell me now?" he asked. "Tell you what?" I inquired. "About you. About us. What exactly were we back then?" he pressed, setting his cup of tea on the table. "I'm not planning on telling you any of that, Thad. You should find out for yourself," I replied firmly.He sighed and then suddenly leaned in closer to me, causing me to lean back in my chair in surprise."What are you doing?" I stammered, feeling a surge of anxiety as memories of my dream resurfaced.He gently touched my hair and revealed a small strand of cloth. "I was trying to take this out," he whispered, his gaze locked onto mine.

His breath brushed gainst my face, sending shivers down my spine."We shouldn't be this close, Thad," I whispered, my voice trembling."I know. What are you thinking about?" he asked, leaning back in his chair, which finally allowed me to release a breath I hadn't realized I was holding."Do you have a boyfriend?" he inquired."No," I replied, shaking my head."But I'm very curious, Sera..." he whispered again, his words hanging in the air, filled with unspoken desire and uncertainty."About what?" I asked, my voice barely above a whisper."Why I'm feeling this way about you," he admitted. "We dated back then, didn't we? We were a couple, and I'm pretty sure we never broke up."His words made my cheeks flush with warmth, and I struggled to find the tight response. "Thad...""I know this may sound weird, but I believe a kiss is all I need to calm my inner turmoil," he continued."What do you mean?" I inquired, still trying to comprehend what he was getting at."I really want to regain my memories, Sera, and I feel like a kiss might be the key. It could help me remember, or it could clear away these confusing feelings," he explained.I couldn't help but scoff. "Do you think this is a 'Sleeping Beauty' situation?""I'm serious," he insisted, his expression earnest. "I'll try anything to regain my memory."I let out a sigh and nodded, my heart racing. "Okay.""Okay? You're giving me the go-ahead to kiss you?" he asked, seeking confirmation, and I nodded again."If you think this is what you need to regain your memory, then go ahead," I said, my voice trembling slightly.He smiled softly and leaned in, hovering over me. His hands slid gently behind my neck, pulling me closer.

I felt my body heat up, and I released a nervous breath, anticipation filling the air.

Chapter 13

Past

I slowly entered his bathroom, softly calling out his name. "Thad, where are you?" I inquired.

He suddenly appeared, pushing me against the wall. "Where have you been? Your mom wants us downstairs," I explained.

He smiled as he leaned in, kissing me softly on the lips. "I don't want to go," he confessed against my lips.

He stepped closer to me, his hard length poking against my leg teasingly.

"what are you doing?" I chuckled as I stared into his eyes. They looked pretty as they have always looked.

"Just enjoying the view," he said, wrapping his arms around me and pulling me against his chest. His erection pressed firmly against my stomach.

With that, he carried me over to the shower stall and gently set me down on one end of it. My eyes twinkle as he took off his shirt, then turned on the water and began rinsing himself off.

"Sera," he said, his voice thick with desire. "I want you so badly."

"Then take me. I am all yours Thad and you know it" I whispered before crashing my lips into his.

The kiss was deep and passionate, tongues swirling together as our passion grew. His hands roamed around my body, caressing skin and exploring curves. Thad broke away from the kiss, breathing heavily. "Oh god...Se ra..."

"You are so beautiful," he groaned, his fingers trailing down the side of my face. Then, he pushed me back against the tiled wall of the shower stall and claimed my mouth once more.

As he pressed his body against mine, his hard length grinding against my lower stomach, i felt a thrill of anticipation course through me and I shook. I wrapped my legs around him and moaned softly into the kiss.

I was getting wet and I could feel it.

Thad pulled away from the kiss and looked into my eyes. "I can't wait any longer," he said roughly, then slid his hands underneath me and lifted me up onto the countertop.

He pressed his lips against mine once more, his tongue tracing the curves of my mouth as his hands explored my body, pushing up my dress and sliding down to my thighs.

I gasped as he slipped a finger inside me, feeling the wet heat of my arousal.

My body was incredibly responsive, arching into his touch. He growled low in his throat, thrusting two fingers deeper inside me. "You're so fucking tight," he murmured against my ear.

I moaned, my head falling back against the cool tile. I wrapped my arms around his neck and pulled him closer, my breathing heavy with desire.

Thad kissed and nipped at my neck, his fingers finding my clit and rubbing softly. I trembled. "I'm going to make you cum so hard," he whispered against my skin.

Without warning, he suddenly spun me around, pushing me up against the wall with my back to his front. He slid his hands up my thighs and hooked them around my waist, then pressed his chest against mine.

I gasped at the sudden change in position, my legs trembling. I could feel every inch of him against me, and the heat between us was almost unbearable. "Thad...," i moaned, arching into him.

Thad groaned, his fingers sliding under the elastic of my panties and pushing them aside. He positioned himself at my entrance, his thick length pressing against my wetness

"Tell me you want this," he growled, his hips starting to move slowly against mine.

I whimpered, my head falling back against the wall. "I want you," i panted, my body trembling with anticipation.

Thad thrust forward, burying himself deep inside of me with one powerful stroke. He let out a low groan as he felt my tight walls squeezing him. "Fuck," he breathed against my ear, starting to move his hips in a slow, steady rhythm.

I cried out my voice resonating in his bathroom, my nails digging into the counter. I could feel every inch of him inside me, filling me up completely. It was intense and overwhelmingly pleasurable.

Thad's movements became faster and harder, his breath hot against my neck.

"You're so tight," he groaned, his hips slamming against mine in a primal rhythm.

My body was wracked with pleasure, my cries echoing through the bathr oom.The wall in front of me provided little cushioning, but the sensation was exquisite.

As his pace quickened, i felt the familiar tingling start at my core. I was close-so close to that blissful release. Thad's hands gripped my hips tighter, his fingers digging into my flesh as he pushed deeper inside of me.

My orgasm hit me like a freight train, my body shuddering with the force of it. I cried out, my voice echoing in the bathroom as i came hard around Thad's cock.

Present

I closed my eyes as his moist lips met mine, a shiver of anticipation coursing through me. He began by gently nibbling on my lower lip, his kisses soft and tender before enveloping my entire mouth with his.

Images from my dream flooded my mind, and I couldn't resist reaching for his hair, running

my fingers through it.

He let out a soft groan against my lips, fueling my desire as I continued to respond to his actions. His movements were deliberate as he leaned in closer,

his hands gliding sensually over my thigh, coaxing me to widen them further.

He continued to trail kisses along my neck, and as I opened my eyes, a soft, involuntary groan escaped my lips. The longing for his touch had always been there, but a sense of caution started to creep in.

"Thad..." I whimpered, my voice barely a whisper as I reluctantly removed my hands from his hair. "We should stop,"

He gradually ceased kissing me and pulled away slowly, a hint of regret in his eyes.

"I'm sorry," he murmured, distancing himself from me. sighed and sat up, adjusting my T-shirt

"It's okay," I reassured him, exhaling slowly. We both sat in an uncomfortable silence. Breaking the tension, I asked, "So, did you regain any memories?"

He shook his head, disappointment evident. "No. I must have been foolish to

think a kiss could bring back memories from years ago," he admitted, standing up.

"I will leave now, I can't stay here tonight anyway," he declared, picking up his phone.

"But how will you get home? I can prepare..." I began to offer help, concern in my voice.

He interrupted me, his tone intense, "I'll call my assistant to bring me a car. Sera, I'm barely holding myself together right now, and I don't know what I

might do if I stay here a few minutes longer."

His words made me gulp nervously, and all I could manage was a quiet, "Goodnight, Thad," as he made his way out of my house.

* * *

"What's going on, Sera? I've been noticing you making unnecessary adjustments to the meal you've been preparing for days now. It's either you're using too many ingredients or too little," Clara remarked, her patience wearing thin.

She quickly took the dough from my hands, assuming control of the situation.

"You can head home; I'll finish the rest on my own. It seems like you're not thinking straight," she insisted.

I whispered back, attempting to take the dough back from her, "No, I can handle it myself."

"Just go home, Sera. If you keep this up, you might scare away all the customers from this restaurant," Clara insisted firmly, refusing to return the dough tome.

I nodded slowly and reluctantly left the kitchen. After cleaning up in the restroom, I couldn't help but dwell on the fact that it had been a week since I last saw Thad.

He hadn't visited the restaurant or my house. Initially, I tried to ignore it, almost relieved, but I couldn't shake off the memory ofthat passionate kiss we shared, and it seemed like he had ignited a long-lost emotion within me that night.

Frustration built within me as I attempted to call Thad, only to realize that i didn't have his contact.

With a heavy sigh, I left the restaurant, holding onto the hope of seeing him there, but he was nowhere to be found.

I made my way to my car, a sense of longing in my heart, and drove out of the parking lot.

* * *

Thad

"I'm sure you're wondering why I invited you to dinner tonight," Callista remarked, her gaze fixed on me. She looked stunning in her outfit and matching heels, although a thought inexplicably crossed my mind that it

would suit Seraphina better.

I let out a sigh, puzzled as to why my mind wandered back to Seraphina once again.

Guilt gnawed at me for that impulsive kiss I shared with her, thinking it might trigger my lost memories and make everything right.

But I was wrong.

If Seraphina hadn't intervened and called me out to stop, I might have taken things further that night right there on the couch.

I found myself becoming a complete mess and losing control whenever I was with her. The desire to touch and be close to her was overwhelming, and I had

initially believed that distancing myself would make these feelings disappear.

Instead, they only grew stronger, leaving me in a state of confusion.

"Yes, it's quite surprising," I admitted, trying to lighten the mood with a soft chuckle.

She smiled in response, perhaps sensing the inner turmoil I was experiencing.

"Thad, who am I to you?" She asked abruptly, catching me off guard.

"Why are you asking me that all of a sudden?" I inquired, puzzled by her question.

"Because I need to know. Not knowing is driving me crazy, so please, just answer," she pleaded, a glimmer of hope in her eyes.

I sighed, "You're my friend, Callie. A very close friend," leaning back in my chair.

"Is that all? Nothing more?" She pressed for clarification.

"What do you mean?" I asked, my confusion deepening.

"You know what I'm talking about, Thad," she said, her words coming out in a rush. "Anyone who's seen the way I act around you and the things I do for you would understand."

She sighed, seeming torn. "I know this might be forward for a lady, but it took me a lot of courage to call you and set up this dinner."

"Callista, what are you..." I began to respond, but she interrupted me

"I like you, Thad. I've always liked you, and I used to think it was because we were close friends in college and did everything together. But now... it's

become something more, something I can't quite define. I like you a lot," she confessed, her gaze fixed on me.

I sat there, my expression blank, even though I had a feeling this moment would come after the night she kissed me. Still, it took me by surprise how soon it had arrived.

"Say something and don't just stare at me like that," she urged, softly taking hold of my right hand that rested on the table.

"Callie, I do understand what you're saying, but I don't..." I began, but she interrupted me.

"If you're thinking of rejecting me, then don't say anything," she interjected firmly. "I'll wait for your answer, Thad. And if you consider rejecting me again, I'll keep pushing and won't give up. I'm prepared for that."

I let out a sigh and gently withdrew my hand from hers.

"Callie, I don't want to hurt you, but please don't expect what you want from me," I said

honestly, meeting her gaze.

She sighed in response. "I know the kind of person you are, Thad. We've been friends for years," she said, determination in her voice. "But I'm not going to change what I said. I'll do my best and never give up."

With a nod, she shifted the conversation. "Shall we order now?" she asked, offering a smile as she signaled the waiter.

Seraphina

I was lounging on my bed, scrolling through my phone when I heard the doorbell chime.

I sat up, perplexed since I wasn't expecting anyone. His face

flickered through my mind, and I promptly got up, rushing towards the door.

I yanked it open, my heart racing, only for my hope to dissipate instantly.

"Lys," I breathed out, looking at him standing there. "You didn't tell me you were coming," I remarked, and he responded with a smile.

"I thought we should have dinner together," he said, holding up both his hands, each filled with a white bag containing pizza, my favorite.

I managed to force a smile and opened the door wider for him to come in.

"Come in," I said, stepping aside as he entered.

"It's pretty chilly outside," he muttered as he headed towards the living room.

I closed the door behind me and followed him. "I can make some tea for you if you'd like," I offered, and he nodded in agreement.

I quietly made my way to the kitchen, pushing thoughts of Thad from my mind for the moment.

"How's work been treating you lately?" I inquired, looking at him as we both sipped our tea.

"It's been fine, you know, the usual files to go through and all," he replied, prompting me to nod in understanding.

Then, he surprised me by suggesting a trip.

"A trip? Where to?" I asked,

setting my tea cup down on the table, my eyes widening in surprise.

"Anywhere you want."

"Anywhere I want?" I repeated, a sense of intrigue piquing my interest.

"But why the sudden urge for a trip?" I inquired, still somewhat puzzled.

"Because it's been ages since we went on one. The last time was back in college, and I think it would be nice if we did it again," he explained, looking at me.

"But it's completely fine if you don't want to go. I just thought it could be good for you."

I sighed and gave him a thoughtful look. "I'm not sure yet, but I'll check my schedule and see if there are any important events this week. If it works

out, maybe I can take a leave from work. Let's see how it goes," I said with
a smile,

considering the idea.

"Okay," he replied with a nod.

I let out a yawn, covering my mouth with my hand.

"You're feeling sleepy already? That's early. Why don't you go to bed, and
I'll take care of this myself?" he suggested, gesturing towards our cups.

"No, I can handle it," I insisted, standing up and picking up the cups. As
I made my way toward the kitchen, I accidentally bumped my leg against
the couch, causing the cups to slip from my hands and shatter on the floor.

"Sera, are you okay?" Lys rushed over to me, concern in his voice.

"I'm fine, I'll just pick these up," I insisted, bending down to retrieve the
broken glass, but Lys was quicker to grab my hand.

"What do you think you're doing? You could get hurt. Let me handle it,"
he said, beginning to pick up the pieces.

I watched him from behind, a rush of memories flooding my mind, memories of Thad in the kitchen, and it left me feeling somewhat conflicted.

I quickly knelt down and joined him in picking up the broken glass,
determined not to think about the similarities between Lys and Thad's
actions.

I had a strange yearning for Thad to be different, to do more for me,
although I couldn't quite explain why I felt that way.

"I just feel uncomfortable letting you do it all by yourself," I explained when
I noticed Lys looking at me with surprise.

He sighed, clearly frustrated. "You really don't listen, Sera," prompting me to force a smile in response.

The absence of Thad for an entire week seemed to be stirring up emotions within me that I hadn't wanted to confront, emotions I hadn't felt in a long time.

Chapter 14

T had "Why is this happening? We finalized the deal with Mr. Norman in Paris four months ago, so why is he changing his mind now?" I questioned Mark,

frustration evident as I slammed my hand on my desk. "He mentioned that he's no longer interested and intends to hand over the project to Wills and Co," Mark replied, his gaze fixed on me. I sighed, my jaw clenched with determination. "Set up an appointment with him for me. I'll go see him tomorrow," I instructed, ready to address this

unexpected turn of events. "I don't think I'll be able to do that, sir," Mark replied, and I looked at him with confusion.

"What do you mean?" "Mr. Norman went back to Paris this morning," he explained, causing me to groan in frustration. "But he should be back soon since we've already started working on the project," I reasoned, taking a seat. "I don't think so, sir. He went there to attend an event, the Callari event," Mark clarified, adding another layer of complexity to the situati on. "Callari? You mean the one they hold once a year in Paris?" I sought confirmation, and he nodded in response. I sighed once more, running my hand through my hair. The Callari event was a gathering of high-status business people, CEOs, and entrepreneurs.Attending it could not only help me convince Mr. Norman but also establish connections with potential business partners for my company."Clear my schedule for the next four days; I'm going to Paris," I instructed, rising from my chair."Okay, sir," Mark acknowledged."Make sure the plane and everything else is prepared," I added."Understood. When are you leaving, sir?" he inquired."Tomorrow morning," I confirmed, determined to make the most of this unexpected opportunity.

SeraphinaI turned off the tap and exited the bathroom, closing the door behind me.After drying off, I put on my underwear and threw on a large T-shirt.Just as I was in the middle of drying my hair with a towel, the doorbell rang.I hurriedly went to answer it, and my surprise was evident when I saw Thad standing there."Thad? What are you doing here?" I questioned, puzzled by his unexpected presence.He looked up at me, desire unmistakably shining in his eyes. "Can I come in?" he asked, and I nodded, allowing him inside."Yes," I breathed out, allowing him to step inside."Why are you here?" I managed to ask after closing the door, but Thad silenced me by passionately crashing his lips into mine, pinning me against the door.I murmured softly against his lips, attempting to convey the need for him to relax, but he remained undeterred, pressing his lips against mine with fervor.His kisses grew more intense, and he quickly, yet gently, lifted my thigh, causing me to instinctively wrap my legs around his waist. As we continued to kiss, he ran his hands over my legs, applying a firm and slightly rough

touch that elicited a passionate moan from me, escaping into his mouth. He planted tender kisses along my neck, causing me to let out a whimper ofpleasure.

"Thad," I whispered, my arms embracing his neck with a fervent grip. He moved with swiftness, carrying me to the couch and gently setting me down, his eyes filled with a contented desire."We probably shouldn't be doing this," I exhaled, my eyes fixed on him as he began to unzip his trousers.

He remained silent, opting to draw one of my thighs closer to him inste ad.Thad," I attempted to speak, but my words dissolved into a passionate moan that slipped past my lips."I need you, Sera," he whispered, his fingers moving deliberately as he slowly pulled down my underwear.I let out a low groan, eagerly spreading my thighs for him, my hands tightly gripping his neck as I drew him in for a passionate kiss."I need you too," I whispered, breaking away from the kiss. He gazed down at me in affection.PresentI slowly opened my eyes, greeted by the gentle morning light streaming into the room. Sitting up, I took in my surroundings, the warmth of the sunlight casting a soft glow.A groan escaped my lips as I ran my fingers through my hair, the realization hitting me that I had yet another vivid dream about Thad."Why does this happen every time I think of him before sleep?" I muttered to myself, my irritation evident in my voice.

"It's not even real," I added, letting out a frustrated sigh.Just then, the doorbell chimed, instantly diverting my attention. I jumped to my feet, Luna, my faithful companion, following closely behind me.I cautiously approached the door, peering through the peephole, and my heart skipped a beat when I saw Thad standing there.

I instinctively pulled

back, taking a step away, and let out an astonished gasp."Why is he showing up here? What could possibly be his reason?" I whispered to myself, feeling a mix of frustration and confusion.

He rang the doorbell once more, and I reluctantly opened the door, cautiously sticking my head outside."Hi," he greeted me, and I couldn't help but notice how handsome he looked in his coat. My gaze wandered to his lips, the same lips I had passionately kissed in my dream just moments ago."Why are you here?" I asked, my curiosity tinged with a touch of caution."I need you..." he began, but I cut him off abruptly, my hand raised in protest."Stop!" I exclaimed. "Don't expect me to say 'I need you too' because I don't. So, whatever's going on in your head, you should stop it now. Nothing is ever going to happen between us," I rambled, my voice filled with determination

as I looked away, avoiding his gaze.Thad appeared puzzled, his confusion evident in his expression. "Are you

okay, Seraphina?" he asked, glancing down at my pajamas."Huh?" I replied, caught off guard by his question."I need you to go on a trip with me. A very important one. What were you thinking?" he clarified, his tone serious and urgent."A trip? Why should I go on a trip with you?" I questioned, my arms folding across my chest."Due to some reasons, but I really need you to come with me now. We don't have much time," he replied urgently, his tone implying the seriousness of the situation.I couldn't help but let out a short laugh. "You want me to go on a trip with you after you kissed me about a week and a half ago and then took off without calling or approaching me?" I pointed out, my frustration evident."About that, Sera, I couldn't..." Thad began to explain."And it seems you're forgetting something here," I interrupted, raising an eyebrow. "I have a job I go to every day, and I need to be there today.""Uhmm... I already took a leave for you," Thad admitted, his eyes avoiding mine."What?!" I exclaimed, my voice filled with a mix of shock and frustration. I hurried inside, making my way to my room to grab my phone, with Thad

following closely behind me.As I checked my phone, a message from Sarah confirmed that I shouldn't come to work for the entire week.

I sighed and set my phone down on my bed before turning to face Th ad."Who do you think you are? Why do you think you can interfere in my work life?" I demanded, my irritation clear in my words."I did you a favor, why are you angry about that? You also need to rest; going to that restaurant every day is not good for your health. You need to change your environment," Thad explained, his tone trying to be reasonable."Or you did it because of your silly trip?" I retorted, my frustration still apparent. I stared him down, waiting for an honest answer."And that too," he admitted softly, his gaze drifting down to my lips. He quickly cleared his throat and took a few steps away from me, his jaw tightening, which left me puzzled.

"But I must say, you look very pretty in the morning," he added, his tone shifting to a more complimentary one.

I sighed, a mix of emotions swirlingnwithin me."Where are we going to? And why do I have to go with you?" I inquired, my arms still folded ."Paris," he replied calmly."Paris?" I exclaimed in disbelief."Yes, I have a very important person to meet there, and I will need you with me," he explained."Need me for what?" I questioned further."By my side, I need you to stay with me over there," he clarified.I looked at him skeptically, as if he had sprouted horns, and scoffed.

"Why do you need me by your side?" I asked, my curiosity piqued."Because that's the only way I would focus!" Thad exclaimed in frustration."I crave for your touch and to have you by my side, Sera. I don't plan on doing anything to you yet, just... come with me before I turn into a mess," he pleaded, running his hands through his hair.I let out a deep sigh, taking in all that he had said. He genuinely seemed to need me with him. This was an opportunity to have him by my side and perhaps spend more time together.

My hesitation started to wane, and I nodded slowly. "Alright, Thad. I'll go with you to Paris.""I will pack and meet you outside. But it would take some time for me to finish up," I explained

"How many minutes?" he inquired."Two hours," I replied, and he blinked a few times, surprised."Okay, I'll be waiting in my car outside," he agreed, and I nodded, already mentally planning what I needed to bring for this unexpected trip to Paris.

Chapter 15

S eraphina

"I can't believe I'm here without Luna. I miss her so much," I said, my gaze fixed on a picture of my dog on my phone.I had been repeating that sentiment over and over since we disembarked from his plane and got into his car, and Thad appeared tired of hearing it.

He let out a sigh.I turned my attention to the window, watching as we approached a large black gate."Are we not staying in a hotel?" I asked, my surprise evident as the gate opened and the driver drove us inside."No, I have my house here, multiple actually, but this one is closer," Thad explained, his fingers moving swiftly on his phone before he looked up at me."Don't worry, it's just for four days," he assured me.I nodded in response, still processing the recent changes in my life. It was surreal to be on a trip with Thad in Paris after not seeing him for years.We disembarked and entered the house, where servants promptly arrived to

collect our luggage."Let me show you to your room," Thad offered, leading the way upstairs, and I followed him, curious about the place where I would be staying for the next few days."Did you prepare this for me?" I asked, taking in the room's décor.

It was undeniably adorable, in an expensive and fancy way, with everything in shades of pink."Yes, girls love pink a lot, so I decided to make it pink," he explained, a glint of pride in his eyes.

I stared at him, feeling a surge of mixed emotions. He had prepared this room for me, but it seemed he had forgotten something

fundamental about me - I actually hated the color pink.

It was a stark reminder that he had forgotten, and our connection wasn't what it used to be."Thanks," I whispered, my voice tinged with a hint of sadness, and he nodded in response."Make yourself at home," Thad said before he left the room, and the servants brought my luggage in.I sighed, feeling a mix of emotions as I settled onto the bed. Thad's situation weighed on my mind, and I found myself yearning for him to regain his

memory, to remember our past and everything about me.Another sigh escaped my lips as I pulled out my phone and messaged Clara, asking her to take good care of Luna.As I lay on the bed, deep in thought, exhaustion took over, and I drifted into sleep without even realizing it.

ThadAfter spending hours working on my laptop, I finally closed it and decided to step out of my room. I anticipated a bit of activity in the living room, perhaps Sera watching a movie or just hanging around.However, as I walked down the quiet hallway towards her room, I began to feel a sense of unease. I let out a sigh and softly knocked on her door while calling her name."Sera! Sera!" I repeated, but there was no response. Concern growing, I knocked a bit louder, yet still, there was no answer. With a sense of trepidation,

I slowly pushed the door open and entered her room.The room was dimly lit, and my gaze immediately went to the bed where I saw Sera. She was fast asleep, curled up on the bed with her hair spread across her face.I walked over to her bed quietly and sat down by her side. With gentle fingers, I brushed the strands of hair away from her face.

She looked so peaceful and innocent in her slumber, and I couldn't help but feel a strange sensation inside me.My eyes were drawn to her lips, and I felt a deep inner turmoil. They seemed to beckon me, and I found it increasingly difficult to control myself whenever I saw them.One thing was becoming increasingly clear to me - I had dated Sera in my past, and despite her reluctance to admit it, we had loved each other.

The mystery of why I had lost my memory of her and how to regain it consumed my thoughts.

As Sera shifted in her sleep, tucking herself closer to me, a soft smile crept onto my face. She was undeniably the kind of woman I would want to date,

and I had a strong hunch that she was the one I had dated before, back in my lost memories."What are you doing to me, Sera?" I whispered, my eyes fixed on her sleeping form. I glanced at the clock and noticed that it was already 10 PM. Judging

by her appearance, it seemed she hadn't taken a bath or eaten yet.Worry gnawed at me, and I gently shook her shoulders, calling her name urgently. "Sera, wake up! Sera!"Her eyes slowly fluttered open, revealing those sparkling green orbs. "Thad?" she said softly, her voice carrying a distinctive quality that always stirred

something inside me, leaving me with a strange and warm feeling."Let's eat dinner," I suggested.Sera groaned softly as I helped her sit up."Dinner?" she asked, sounding drowsy, and I nodded."I'm not eating tonight; I feel so sleepy," she protested, attempting to settle back on the bed. However, I was quick to hold her and gently pull her back up."I'm not letting you sleep without eating," I insisted, shaking her lightly.She sighed and reluctantly agreed, "Okay, let go of me." I promptly released my hold on her shoulders, determined to make sure she had a proper meal

before resting.I stood up and took a step away from her bed as she attempted to stand.

However, her legs seemed to give out, causing her to slump down. Without thinking, I reached out and grabbed her by the waist, pulling her close to me.It was in that moment that I realized how small her waist was."Are you okay? What's wrong with you?" I asked, genuine concern evident in my voice as I helped her sit back on the bed.She chuckled and looked up at me. "It's because I just woke up. My legs always feel like jelly when I get up suddenly. You must have forgotten that too," she explained, and I regarded her with a puzzled expression."What do you mean?" I asked, but she just forced a smile."Nothing. I need to freshen up; I'll meet you downstairs," she said, and I nodded slowly before leaving her room. Her words left me with a sense of

unease, as if there was more to our past that I couldn't remember."Her legs feel like jelly anytime she wakes up? Why don't I remember hearing

this before?" I muttered to myself, puzzled by the new piece of information as I descended the stairs.

SeraphinaI examined myself in the mirror, wearing a large T-shirt and shorts with my damp hair slightly tousled. A soft smile crept onto my face as I contemplated my presence here."I still can't believe I'm here," I whispered to myself before grabbing my phone and heading downstairs.Upon reaching the dining area, I found Thad engrossed in his phone, and the table was set with food ready to be eaten.

I cleared my throat to get his

attention, and he looked up at me."Finally, I thought you had gone back to bed again," he remarked with a small chuckle.I was about to sit down when

I noticed his expression change. His eyes widened slightly, and he pointed his fork casually in the direction of my thigh."You still have that tattoo?" he asked, his tone casual. I froze, slowly turning to look at him, and I could see shock overtaking his face when he realized what he had just said."How did you know I have a tattoo there?" I asked, my gaze locked onto his.

"Because... we both got it together," he whispered, and a gasp escaped my

mouth as his words hung in the air, leaving me in stunned silence.Tears welled up in my eyes as I continued to stare at him, overwhelmed by the flood of emotions that his memory of the tattoo brought back."How did you..." I began to ask, but he interrupted softly,

"I don't know how,

but I just suddenly remembered it now." The rest of dinner passed in silence, neither of us broaching the topic again.I was happy that he remembered something about the tattoo, but I hadn't expected him to recall it and the associated memories. It left me feeling both relieved and apprehensive about what else might resurface.As I absentmindedly scrolled through my phone, my gaze drifted to Thad, who was focused on his laptop. I couldn't help but admire his features.

He had grown into a very handsome man, and the sight of him filled me with a sense of happiness.

Memories of my dreams flooded my mind, causing my heart to beat a bit faster. Lost in my thoughts, I didn't realize that he had looked up and caught me staring at him.

It was too late to avert my gaze, so we found ourselves locked in a silent gaze, our eyes meeting in a moment of unspoken connection."Can I go to the balcony... for fresh air?" I whispered, my voice slightly trembling.He nodded slowly, still keeping his gaze locked on me. Without wasting any time, I stood up and hurriedly made my way out of the living room to the balcony.

My thoughts raced as I closed the door behind me, realizing that

coming to Paris with Thad might have been a colossal mistake, as I found it increasingly difficult to control my emotions when I was around him.

***

The next morning, I went through my usual morning routine, getting dressed before heading downstairs. To my surprise, I found Thad already dressed in

his coat."Good morning," I greeted him."Good morning," he responded, his eyes showing a flicker of surprise as he took in my outfit before quickly regaining his composure."Are you going somewhere?" "Yes, to work. I'll be back late in the night, so you can call me if you need anything," he explained."But I don't have your contact, and didn't you say you need me by your side? Is that not why you brought me here?" I questioned."I did say that, but what I meant is..." he started."It's fine. Put your number in here," I said, extending my phone to him.

He sighed and accepted it, typing a few buttons before returning it to me.I glanced at the screen and gasped when I saw what he had saved his number as. "Why did you save your number as 'boyfriend'? You're not my boyfriend,"

I exclaimed, a mix of surprise and amusement in my voice."Well, I was, and I still am because we never broke up from what I can remember in my head," Thad explained, lightly tapping his head with his index finger.A spark of hope flared within me, and I couldn't help but ask, "Have you regained your memory?""Just a little, and I remembered quite a lot of things," he replied with a smirk, making me gulp nervously."But still... you can't just save your name as 'my boyfriend,'" I challenged him, but he didn't seem interested in continuing the conversation.

He turned and walked away, leaving me with a whirlwind of thoughts and emotions."Thad!" I called out, making him turn to look at me."What did you remember?" I asked, my voice trembling slightly."Do you really want me to say it?" he responded, his voice husky as he walked back toward me.

I took a step back as his gray eyes bore into mine."Yes," I whispered, my curiosity getting the better of me.

He leaned in close, his breath tickling my left ear as he whispered, "You definitely don't want to know, but I must say that you have grown into a very

beautiful lady, princess." He pulled back slightly, looking at me to gauge my reaction.I stood there in shock, frozen by his words. He had just called me "Princess," a nickname he used to give me when we were dating."See you tonight," he said before turning and walking away, leaving me standing there, still processing what had just happened."He called me 'Princess,'" I whispered to myself, a smile spreading across my

face.

It had been so long since I had heard anyone call me that, and in that moment, I felt tears of happiness trickle down my cheek.

His memory was slowly coming back, and it filled me with hope and joy.

Chapter 16

P ast

"What? Princess?" I asked, my eyes locked onto his gray ones as he lay casually on his bed, hands behind his head, resting on them.

"Yes. I love the nickname, and moreover, that's what you are to me.Don't you like it?" he inquired.

"I do. I love it," I replied with a small smile.

"You have to because I'm not changing it," he declared before pulling me close to his chest. I chuckled and wrapped my arms around his waist.

"I love you, Sera," he whispered, giving me a gentle peck on the head.

Present

I sat down by the edge of the pool, my hands resting by my sides as I gazed up at the sky. The stars illuminated the night, casting a sparkling glow as they dotted the expanse of the sky.

I released a contented sigh and redirected my attention to the pool, my feet kicking playfully through the water, causing splashes to dance in the moonlight.

"He said he was going to be back tonight," I murmured, my gaze shifting towards the direction of the door.

With a sigh, I retrieved my phone from my side and glanced at the time, noting that it was already 8pm.

"It's getting late," I said once more, locking my phone and setting it down on the floor beside me.

My phone buzzed beside me and I reached for my it, its screen lighting up with Ly's name. A smile naturally found its way to my lips as I answered.

"Senior," I greeted him softly, the warmth of his presence evident in my tone.

"What are you up to?" Ly's voice came through the phone, filled with curiosity.

"Not much, just some casual sky gazing," I replied, unsure of how to describe my current activity.

A soft chuckle echoed through the line, and I couldn't help but smile even wider.

"I'll be coming to your place tomorrow," Ly informed me.

"My place?" I echoed in surprise.

"Yeah?" Ly confirmed.

I sighed and ran a hand through my face, realizing that I hadn't informed him about my current trip.

"Actually, Lys, I'm not at home right now," I whispered into the phone, my voice barely above a hush.

"What do you mean? Did you go to your mom's house?" he inquired, a touch of concern in his tone.

"No, not that," I began, stammering slightly. "I'm actually on a trip. It's kind of like a business trip, but not really. It's more like a vacation, you know nothing too stressful."

A brief pause hung in the air.

"It's okay as long as you're safe. So, where are you?" Lys asked, his voice filled with curiosity.

"Paris," I replied.

"That's quite a long journey, Sera. Did you go with Clara?" Lys wondered.

"No, it's a bit more complicated," I explained, making vague gestures with my hand. "I'll tell you all about it when I get back."

"Alright. Have fun and stay safe, Sera. Let me know if anything comes up or

if you need..." Lys started to say.

"Okay, okay. Goodbye for now," I interjected, already accustomed to his

caring nature.

I ended the call and smiled at my phone's screen, appreciating

his concern.

I heard soft footsteps and turned my head to witness a shadow slowly making its way back into the house.

In a hurry, I withdrew my leg from the water and rose to my feet. With quick strides, I headed back inside and found Thad already ascending the stairs.

"Thad!" I called out, and he halted in his tracks, turning to face me.

His eyes appeared a shade darker than usual, and faint bags were etched

beneath them. He looked visibly drained, his exhaustion evident.

"Are you okay?" I inquired, approaching him. I paused a foot away from him

on the steps.

He managed a tired smile.

Suddenly, he lowered his head onto my shoulder and wrapped his arms

around my waist, drawing me into an embrace.

I gasped slightly in surprise at his unexpected action.

"Thad..." I began.

"I missed you and your scent," he whispered, his warm breath brushing against my neck, sending an unexpected surge of warmth through me.

I exhaled shakily, the scent of his cologne lingering around me. My hands

found their way to his back, gently patting it in response to his embrace.

"Was work stressful today?" I inquired, my voice soft and full of concern.

"Not really. I just missed you," he whispered once more.

A warm, genuine smile appeared on my lips, as if we were in a real relationship in that moment. I cherished the cozy atmosphere and wished it could last longer, though I knew it wouldn't.

Someday, everything would change.

We remained like that for a few more precious minutes before he eventually let go. His gray eyes rested on my face, faintly twinkling.

"I should head upstairs now. I need to get some sleep," he said, and I nodded in understanding.

He turned and made his way up the stairs, walking until he reached the hallway leading to his room.

I gently closed the door behind me and wandered over to my bed, taking a seat.

"Should I go check on him?" I whispered, uncertain about visiting him in his room at this late hour.

With a sigh, I rested my head on the bed.

"Let's just go to bed, Sera," I murmured, attempting to push my worries for him to the side.

* * *

Thad

I slowly opened my eyes, catching a whiff of smoke in the air. My surroundings were a blur, and I realized I was still on my bed, trapped in a room that was now ablaze.

I gasped, fear seizing me, and hastily tossed the blankets aside, pushing myself upright.

"Sera!" I called out desperately, frantically searching for an escape route.

The room was enveloped in flames.

The door creaked open slightly, revealing Sera on the other side, wearing a small, sinister smile.

"Sera, what's happening..." I began, my confusion and shock mounting.

"You brought this upon yourself, Thad," she uttered, breaking into a chilling

laughter.

"What?" I whispered, struggling to breathe as the smoke thickened.

A shadowy figure appeared behind her, wrapping his arms around her waist.

"Goodbye!" she said, coldly, and slammed the door shut, leaving me inside, gasping for air.

"Sera!" I screamed before collapsing to the floor, clutching at my own throat as

the choking smoke filled my lungs, my vision fading as the flames consumed

the room.

"Thad!"

I was jolted awake by someone urgently calling my name.

The voice started faint but gradually grew clearer, pulling me from the depths of a nightmare.

My eyes snapped open, and there stood Sera, her face etched with concern. I

was drenched in sweat, my heart racing, and the memory of the fire still vivid in my mind.

"It's just a bad dream, Thad. Just a dream," Sera murmured gently. She moved to sit beside me on the bed, and with a compassionate look in her eyes, she pulled me into a comforting hug, running her fingers soothingly through my hair.

"Sera..." I croaked out, wrapping my arms around her waist. A profound chill

had settled in my bones, making me shiver more than I ever had.

"It's just a dream," she repeated softly, her comforting touch and words offering solace as I struggled to calm my racing heart and ease the cold dread that lingered.

* * *

Seraphina

I dipped the cloth into the bowl of cool water and gently wrung it out beforeplacing it on his forehead.

I had been on my way downstairs to fetch a glass of water when I heard his cries emanating from his room. Thad rarely had nightmares, but when he did, I was always there to comfort him.

The realization hit me like a wave of guilt. How had he coped when I wasn'tthere, and he had no one to chase away the nightmares? Thad had oftentold me that I was the only one capable of soothing his night terrors, and byleaving, I felt like I had betrayed him.

My gaze drifted to Thad's sleeping face, and he appeared as innocent as he had ever been. His eyes were gently closed, long eyelashes resting on hischeekbones, while his nose retained its straight, familiar shape.

My attention was then drawn to his lips, tempting me to trace my fingers over them. His right hand clung tightly to mine, refusing to let go, even in his sleep.

Thad had grown into a remarkably handsome man, much like the one Iknew back then. It pained me to realize I wasn't there with him through histransformation.

The fear of him regaining memories of the accident that night gnawed at myheart. I feared he might leave me or demand never to see me again when hediscovered that I was the cause of the accident and his memory loss.

"I'm sorry," I whispered, leaning in to plant a gentle kiss on his forehead, myheart heavy with regret.

My feelings for him hadn't waned, I knew that much. It had been there allalong, quietly persisting, but I never mustered the courage to seek him out.

And now, here he was, right beside me, clinging to me. Yet, I still lacked thestrength to tell him the truth: that we had a terrible fight the night he had hisaccident.

Chapter 17

I opened my eyes slowly and noticed that the room was dimly lit. I scanned

my surroundings and realized I was on Thad's bed in his room.

How had I ended up here?Swiftly, I threw off the blankets and hurried to the door, flinging it open. As I descended the stairs, I was met with the sight of Thad, dressed in sweatpants, his back to me.He was busy making coffee and hummed as he worked, a habit he often

indulged in while cooking. My eyes couldn't help but trace the outline of

his broad back, and I noticed a new addition - a large bird tattoo.

It was a mermaid tattoo that had been there before.I descended the stairs with deliberate, soft steps, my gaze firmly fixed on

Thad's bare back.

When he suddenly turned to face me, his grey eyes locked onto mine, and my breath caught.His damp black hair glistened, tiny droplets cascading down from his forehead, tracing a wet path across his cheek, neck, and chest. His six-pack abs seemed as if they had been chiseled out, far more toned than I remembered

from the past.

He had always been a fitness enthusiast, but now his physique seemed even more sculpted.A wave of warmth washed over me, and my heart raced a bit faster."Good morning," he greeted me, a small smirk playing on his lips, his eyes

sparkling.I cleared my throat and nodded. "How... how are you feeling?" I inquired, my voice trembling slightly."As energetic as ever," he replied, his gaze unwavering, creating an electric

tension between us.My heart raced as I nodded and proceeded with caution toward the fridge.The room's dim lighting made Thad's silhouette a shadowy presence, engrossed in his coffee and humming softly.I retrieved a bottle of water from the fridge and filled a glass. My composureslipped as I sensed Thad's gaze bearing down on me. He interrupted my

thoughts, his deep voice breaking the silence, "Would you like some?"I turned slowly, finding myself face to face with him. His intense gaze seemed

to penetrate my very soul. A barely audible whisper escaped my lips, "No, I'm fine, thank you."His closeness was overwhelming, and I sensed his warm breath on my neck

as he offered to make me coffee. I was frozen, unable to move as I felt his

presence envelop me entirely.His penetrating grey eyes locked onto mine, and I could feel the intense heat

of his gaze. My own eyes darted over the familiar lines of his face, tracing

the contours I once knew so well.

A shiver of temptation ran through me,

but I willed myself to pull away, shaking my head.Coughing slightly to hide my inner turmoil, I tightened the cap on the bottle and returned it to the table.

I reached for the cup of water and, with an urgency I couldn't quite contain, downed a large gulp to quell the rising heat within me."Did you...how did I get to the bed?" I asked, looking at him."I carried you," he whispered, taking a slow sip of his coffee. His words hung

in the air, leaving me momentarily startled. Blinking to clear my thoughts, I decided to break the tension and move past him."Aren't you going to work?" I inquired, turning to face him.His eyes met mine, and he shook his head. "No, I'm not. I plan to stay at home with you and unravel the mysteries of our past that you want to keep buried."His answer caught me off guard, and I quickly turned to walk away.Behind me, I heard his soft chuckle, sending a shiver down my spine as I climbed the stairs.

Thad

I had just finished talking to some clients when Mark called me. I picked

up my phone and stood up, moving to the window to take the call."Hello," "Mr. Whitlock, the date of the event has been pushed forward. It's tonight,"

Mark's voice said hurriedly.As I glanced out the window, I saw Sera practicing yoga on the lawn. She

was graceful and focused, her chestnut hair falling across her face, and her

workout attire clinging to her, accentuating her curves."The Callari event?" I inquired to confirm."Yes, sir," She gracefully shifted into another pose, her body arching towards the sky, and I found myself unable to look away.

Memories of the past began to flood

my mind, and I couldn't help but wonder if I truly had the privilege of having her all to myself back then. "Alright, I'll prepare for it," I said before ending the call, my gaze still lingering

on Sera's figure. Feelings for her swelled up inside me, a yearning I hadn't anticipated. It

seemed like I needed her with me all the time.

The nightmare I had just

experienced was centered around her, and it hurt to imagine another man in

her company while I was consumed by flames. Her comforting hug had felt warm and strangely familiar, as if she had always

been the one to console me during nightmarish moments.

I tried to hide my lingering gaze as she turned in my direction, clearing my throat and walking away from the window, conscious that I'd been caught

Chapter 18

P^{ast}

Lying beside Thad on his bed, I could feel the warmth of his touch as he traced his fingers gently over my stomach. I wore a crop top and shorts, and his gaze was fully focused on me, making my heart race.

"How many children do you want?" he asked, the vulnerability in his eyes matching his gentle touch.

"Three," I whispered, my gaze locked onto the ceiling of his room.

"Three?" Thad repeated, his fingers shifting my face toward him briefly.

"Yes, two girls and a boy," I replied.

"Why?" he inquired, his curiosity evident.

"What do you mean?" I asked, unsure of where he was going with this.

"Why two girls and not two boys?" he pressed.

"Because... the boys will all look like you, and I don't want pesky girls chasing my boys around," I replied with a playful pout.

He chuckled, his eyes dancing with amusement.

"So you just admitted that I'm handsome, huh?" he teased, moving his hands from my stomach to cup my face.

"No, I didn't," I said, though I knew I had slipped up.

He laughed and kissed me softly.

"I'm fine with any child you want, Sera, as long as you're their mother," he murmured against my lips.

"Who said anything about marrying you, Thad?" I said, playfully pulling away.

"You're joking," he said, his gaze fixed on me.

"No, I'm not," I replied, holding back a laugh.

"You're going to marry me, whether you like it or not, Seraphine. Believe me, I will shred any man that comes near you into pieces. Only I..." he stopped, pointing to his chest. "Get to marry you and possess you."

I burst into laughter before pulling him in for a hug.

"Okay, okay, anything you want," I said, my voice muffled against his neck.

PresentAs i wrapped up my yoga session, my phone chimed, and I quickly picked

it up, a smile forming on my face as I saw the caller ID."Hey," I greeted cheerfully

Is he that handsome and good in bed that you can't even remember to call your friend, huh?" Clara's voice boomed through the phone.I laughed. "I'm so sorry. How's Luna?" I asked, already missing my dog."She's fine. Now tell me, what's he like? Is he taking care of you really well?

What's his name? Is he...""One question at a time, Clara," I interjected, still chuckling."Just tell me everything now. I want to know who he is," she insisted."I'll explain it all to you when I get back," I reassured her.She groaned audibly on the other end.

"You won't believe it!" she exclaimed."Believe what?" I inquired."Tyler broke up with that girl from the hotel," she revealed with a hint of

satisfaction."The one from the hotel?" I confirmed."Yeah," she replied. "I'm sure he'll be running back to me anytime now.""And you're chasing him away," I added. "Because I'm not allowing you near

that guy anymore."She chuckled. "Don't you trust me?""No, I don't," I retorted, referencing how she had cried and locked herself

away when he cheated on her.

"Whatever. Just stay safe and come home quickly. I miss you," she ranted,

making me laugh."Okay," I replied before we both said our goodbyes and ended the call.Thad interrupted my yoga session, and I turned to see him approaching with

a cloth covering his body, which unfortunately meant I couldn't admire his abs at that moment."When will you be done?" he questioned."Done with what?" I replied, still caught up in my exercises."When will you be done posing like a stripper? I need to make a dish, and I

need your help," he stated, standing in front of me and casting a shadow that blocked the sunlight.I stood up quickly. "I'm done," I muttered and reached for my yoga mat. But Thad was swift to grab it from my grasp."I can do that myself," I mumbled, though I wasn't sure if he heard me, as he had already turned and started walking back into the house.* * *

"You keep doing it the wrong way. This is what I did," I said, raising my

voice slightly as I stood up from the stool and approached Thad, pushing him gently.We were in the kitchen, and he wanted to bake pastries. I'd been trying to

teach him in the simplest way possible, but the counter was filled with wastedflour, which was getting on my nerves, and I'd been raising my voice out of

frustration."This is the way it's meant to be done, not the other way around," I explained

as I rolled the dough smoothly."That's because you're a chef," Thad mum bled."No, you were good at this before. How did you get so bad?" I asked, still

focused on the dough."That's because you weren't here to teach me, so I forgot," he said, and I froze for a moment.Clearing my throat, I reached for his wrist and pulled him closer."Let me teach you again," I whispered, my voice soft as I felt his cologne

surrounding me.I held his right hand and used it to show him the correct way to handle the

dough."It should be done like this; it's easier to learn," I whispered, but I could sense his gaze on my face.He suddenly closed the distance between us, trapping me against the counter, my back turned to him as he covered my figure." Then teach me how to use both of my hands to do it," he whispered, his

breath gently grazing my ear.I cleared my throat and took both of his hands, guiding them over the dough.I began to move his hands slowly at first, gradually increasing the pace, andhis chest pressed against my back. The situation was making me feel warm,

and my mind started wandering to silly thoughts.* * *

Thad"We should stop," she suddenly said, pulling her hands away from mine.

I was enjoying the closeness, the scent of her hair and body, making me feel

warm.

But she turned, and her eyes widened when she saw how close we

were. My gaze dropped to her lips, and I slowly leaned in, hoping to kiss her.However, she quickly evaded me, her nose bumping into mine."I should... go," she whispered, pushing my right hand away and stumbling

forward.I watched her walk away, a small smirk on my lips. It was clear that she was

affecting me as much as I was affecting her."Sera!" I called out, making her stop in her tracks."I have an important dinner event tonight, and I'd like you to come with me,"I said, hopeful that she would agree.

She quickly nodded and hurriedly walked out of the kitchen without looking back at me.I smiled before turning to look at the mess we'd made in the kitchen.One thing was certain: my feelings for Sera had spiraled out of control, and

I had lost all sense of restraint.

Nevertheless, I didn't care. My only desire was to be with her, regardless of whether she was a part of my past or my future. As long as she remained by my side, I felt complete.

SeraphinaI looked at my reflection in the mirror, a satisfied smile on my face. I knew

that Thad's business world often involved events like this.

I had chosen a stunning black gown that gracefully hugged my curves, its body-contouring design accentuating my silhouette. The subtle leg slit added a touch of allure to my outfit.I slipped into a pair of elegant stiletto heels that perfectly complemented the

gown, adding to the overall elegance.

To complete the look, I adorned myself

with delicate diamond stud earrings that shimmered in the soft light.I grabbed my phone and a matching purse, feeling confident with my look,

before making my way out of my room."Are you..." Thad began to ask but paused, his eyes locked on me. He scanned my attire, and I noticed his gaze lingering on my exposed thigh. His jaw tightened for a moment, revealing his intense focus."Yes, I'm all set," I assured him as I approached. Thad nodded and swiftly held the door open for me, allowing me to step out.* * *

Thad"I'd like us to revisit the project, Mr. Norman. We've refined our approach,

and I believe it's worth considering again," I explained, taking a sip of wine

from my glass.

I had spent an hour with him, trying to persuade him, all while stealing glances at Sera.She was radiant and captivating the entire event, seemingly oblivious to my presence.

Currently, she was engaged in lively conversation with some other

ladies, sharing laughter and stories. Her outfit was utterly enchanting, and I

couldn't help but admire her from a distance."Alright, Mr. Whitlock, tell me more," Mr. Norman responded with a hint of

weariness in his voice. His white hair shimmered under the chandelier's light

in the hall."We've bolstered our team, refined project management, and customized our approach to align with the project's unique requirements," I began."What about the concerns we discussed over the phone?" he inqu ired."We've made quality control a top priority and increased transparency in

reporting. You have nothing to worry about," I reassured him.A faint smile crossed Mr. Norman's face. "Now I understand why your

company is thriving and considered one of the best, Mr. Whitlock. I

appreciate your efforts. Let's give it another shot," he said, extending his

hand for a handshake. I firmly shook his hand and returned his smile.It had been 20 minutes since the event concluded, and I couldn't wait to leave,

especially with Sera by my side.

I headed to the balcony, hoping to find her there.

To my surprise, she was

engaged in a phone call on speaker, her laughter filling the silent night."I've missed you so much, Senior," her gentle voice resonated.Senior? Who was she talking to?"Then come back quickly, so we can go on our trip when you're done with

yours," a deep voice replied, clearly belonging to a man.

The realization hit me hard - she was planning a trip with another man. It

bothered me more than it should have.

Why did I care? Who was he? When

were they planning this?Folding my hands into fists, I clenched my jaw. Sera's laughter at something

the guy said felt like a stab, and I couldn't understand why I was so annoyed.I wanted to be the sole reason for her smiles, her happiness. It was irrational,

and I had no right to feel this way.I wanted to be the only person she desired, the only one who touched her,

who undressed her. But that wasn't the reality."Thad?"Sera's voice pulled me from my turbulent thoughts, and I looked up to see her approaching. She held her phone in hand, and I couldn't help but glance at it."Are we leaving now?" she asked, her eyes searching my face.I nodded, trying to mask the hurt that had crept in."Yes, we should go now. It's late," I replied before turning away and walking, not wanting her to see the turmoil in my eyes.

Chapter 19

S eraphina

I slipped my heels off, setting them aside, and took a seat on the couch. Thad had entered the room, closing the door behind him. I sensed something was wrong from the moment we left the event.He had avoided eye contact with me, giving curt responses to my questions.

His behavior was disconcerting.As he walked past me, I reached out and grabbed his hand, making him turn

to face me."Is something bothering you?" I asked, concerned about his unusual behavior."What do you mean?" he replied, his tone guarded."You've been acting strange ever since we left the party. Did something happen there that I should know about?" I inquired, releasing my grip on his wrist.He looked at me for a moment, then let out a bitter chuckle."Is this a performance for fun, or are you just pretending?" he asked, taking a step closer to me.Confused, I began to respond, "What...""Senior, or whatever his name is - the man you're going on a trip with. It

seems like he can make you happier than I can," he interrupted, his gaze locked onto mine."You overheard my conversation?" I asked, taken aback by his confession."Yes, I did. Is there something wrong with that?" Thad replied, his tone still

filled with frustration.A smile crept across my face as I realized that Thad was jealous. It had been so long since I had seen him like this."Lys is my friend, and 'Senior' is just a nickname I use for him most of the

time," I explained, trying to alleviate his concerns.

"A friend? Then why are you going on a trip with him? And a man, at that?"

he responded, raising his voice."I don't plan to go with him, Thad. I have to return to work. Besides, aren't

you also a man?" I asked, still somewhat amused by his reaction."This... is different. We've known each other for a long time, even if you

refuse to admit it, and you are safe with me, Seraphina. But with him, it could

be dangerous," he expressed, gesturing with his hands."But I've known him for a long time too, since college," I replied with a grin,

playfully.Thad sighed in frustration and ran his hand through his hair. His demeanor

shifted, and he became more serious."This is not a joke, Sera," he whispered, closing the distance between us. His

eyes bore into mine with intensity, and I quickly lost my smile."Thad, I'm not going on a trip with him. I am serious, and we are nothing

more than friends," I reassured him, my voice gentle as I felt his cologne enveloping me."So... what about us?" he asked, and I looked at him, a bit bewildered."What?" I inquired."You and me... what are we, Sera? You know how you affect me. You make me

feel like I'm losing my mind, and I feel incomplete when you're not around. I

yearn for your touch, your scent, and everything about you drives me wild,"

he admitted, his words close to my face.I let out a shaky breath as I felt a warmth spread through my body.

"Thad, I think you're getting something wrong," I began, but he interrupted ed

me."No, you're the one refusing to admit that you're feeling the same way I am,"

he insisted, causing me to fall silent. He was right, I couldn't deny the feelings

I had for him. They had always been there, but they had intensified with his

return."I want you, Sera. I always have, and I'm not afraid to say it. Tell me, do you

want me too? Do you... feel the same way I do?" he asked, his voice softening ing

towards the end.I struggled to find the right words as my breathing grew unsteady. My gaze

locked onto his lips, and before I could respond, he surprised me by crashing ing his lips into mine.At first, I was taken aback by his sudden kiss, but I couldn't resist the

magnetic pull between us. I found myself wanting more, and without

hesitation, I wrapped my arms around his neck, drawing him closer.We continued to passionately lock our mouths together, savoring every

moment of the intense kiss.

He swiftly wrapped his strong arms around my thighs and lifted me off the ground. I instinctively encircled my legs around his waist, which caused my gown to ride up, revealing more of my thigh.

Our passionate kiss persisted as he carried me slowly into the room, nudging the door open with his foot.He gently lowered me onto the bed, and with a sensual urgency, he began

to undo my gown, revealing my body inch by inch. My heart raced as the full

realization of what we were about to do set in.In that moment, I didn't care about anything else. I eagerly reached for the

buttons on his shirt, and he obligingly pulled it off, unveiling his chiseled

chest, which felt solid and strong beneath my touch.

We continued to kiss passionately, lost in our world of desire and longing.

I was now dressed in my bra and underwear, and he pulled away to look

at me with delight. "You're even more beautiful than I had imagined," he whispered in a hoarse voice.

Slowly, he reached for my bra and skillfully unhooked it, letting it fall to the floor.I let out a sigh as he removed my bra, exposing my breasts to him. He took

one in each hand and began to massage them softly, his fingers moving back

and forth over my nipples.It sent shivers down my spine, and I could feel myself getting more aroused

by the second. He brought his head closer to mine and kissed me again, our

tongues dancing together in a passionate embrace.I could taste myself on his lips, and I loved it. He moved his mouth lower

and began kissing my neck, making me moan with pleasure."Oh Thad! We..." I trailed off against his mouth."Shh!!" He said with a smile as he kissed my cheek and then my ear.His warm breath tickled my ear, sending shivers of pleasure down my spine.

He moved his mouth to my breast, gently sucking on my nipple while his

hand expertly kneaded the other.

I couldn't help but moan loudly, arching my back in a desperate attempt to feel more of his warm mouth on me.He moved his mouth to my breast, tenderly sucking on my nipple. I gasped with pleasure, but he stopped suddenly and looked at me with a hint of

adoration in his eyes. "You're so beautiful," he whispered, leaning in to kiss me again, our tongues dancing together in a passionate embrace.I moaned against his mouth as he pushed me back onto the bed. He knelt

on the floor between my legs, gazing at me with hunger in his eyes. I released

a shaky breath and willingly spread my legs apart.

I yearned for more of him, more than I ever thought possible. He leaned forward and kissed me softly before taking my left leg and placing

it on his shoulder.

I moaned as he moved his mouth to my inner thigh, showering it with kisses and gentle bites.I could feel goosebumps forming on my skin as he teased me with his tongue.

I arched my back and moaned as he moved to the other side, repeating the

same tantalizing process on my right leg.I could feel the heat building inside me as he moved his mouth towards my

most intimate area. I knew that I was already soaked from the foreplay, but I

wanted more.

I parted my legs wider and raised my hips slightly, inviting him in. He stood

up, and I watched as he unzipped his pants and let them drop to the floor.He was wearing boxers, and I could see the bulge growing underneath the

fabric. He looked at me and smiled. I smiled back, biting my lip, craving his

touch.He got on top of me, his eyes filled with desire. Our lips met in a deep kiss,

and I wrapped my arms around him, pulling him closer, savoring the feeling

of his body against mine.

He broke the kiss and looked into my eyes. "I'm going to take you now," his voice, husky with desire, whispered, and I nodded slowly, surrendering to the intense connection between us.He lifted himself up and positioned himself above me. With a sense of

anticipation and desire, he gently grabbed my panties and slid them off me, baring the essence of our intense intimacy.I was now fully exposed under him, and I eagerly wrapped my legs around

his waist. He lowered himself down, and I felt the intense connection between us. His hands moved to my back, pulling me even closer to him, igniting the passionate embrace that awaited us.My moans grew louder as he entered me, his movements slow and

deliberate, letting me feel every inch of him as he filled me completely. I couldn't hold back my moans as my nails dug into his back, and his own

moans reverberated against my neck. His hands found my breasts, squeezing

them gently as he increased the pace, thrusting deeper and harder, sending

waves of pleasure through my body.Our passion intensified as I moaned louder, my nails digging deeper into

his back. I tightened my legs around his waist, and his own moans grew more

fervent as he continued to thrust into me.

My desire was overwhelming, and I couldn't help but bite down on his shoulder, causing him to cry out in

pleasure.As I approached the peak of my pleasure, he suddenly stopped, leaving me confused and wanting more. He sat up and kissed me passionately, pushing me down onto the bed.He climbed over me and straddled my chest, his strong hands holding mywrists above my head, leaving me completely at his mercy. I couldn't move, all I could do was gaze up at him with anticipation.

He leaned forward, capturing one of my nipples with his mouth, sending shivers of pleasure through my body.He sucked on my nipple while his hips moved with increasing urgency,

sliding in and out of me. I could hear his ragged breaths, matching the tempo

of his thrusts. I moaned in ecstasy, arching my back as I longed for him to go even deeper.We lay there, entwined, still catching our breath. His weight pressed against

me, and I could feel him inside me, pulsing with the aftermath of our passion.Our bodies were slick with sweat, and I couldn't help but smile, savoring the

closeness we'd just shared.He moved away from me and collapsed on the bed beside me, both of us

panting heavily. Our eyes met, and a deep connection seemed to pass between us.

Chapter 20

The soft morning light gently streamed in through the curtains, casting a

warm glow on the room, slowly coaxing me from my peaceful slumber.

I blinked my eyes open to find myself lying face to face with Thad. His

breathing, a soothing and steady rhythm, brushed against my face, wrapping me in a comforting embrace of closeness.

Recollections of the previous night resurfaced in my mind, evoking a myriad of emotions. It had been a considerable amount of time since I had felt the way I did with Thad.

The connection we shared had deepened significantly,

leaving me in a state of both delight and uncertainty.

My gaze was drawn to his long lashes resting gently on his high cheekbones

and then down to his tranquil lips, part of which was obscured by a curtain

of his dark hair.

He lay on his stomach, basking in the soft morning light that gracefully danced across his broad back.

A tender smile played on my lips as I couldn't help but admire him, my heart

swaying with the deep affection I held for him. I've loved him for as long

as I could remember, and his innocent slumber stirred emotions within me,

emotions that had only grown stronger over time.

Cautiously, I began to sit up, the idea of waking him feeling both exciting

and daunting. The previous night had been a mix of tenderness and intimacy,

and I wasn't quite ready to face the morning just yet.

I tried to gently ease his hands away from my waist, silently praying not to

disturb his peaceful sleep. With my heart pounding in my chest, I succeeded and slipped off the bed, although not without a minor mishap-my backside inadvertently bumped into the floor, causing a slight wince.

Hoping I hadn't roused him, I stole a glance at his still-sleeping form, and my anxiety eased when I saw he remained undisturbed. Clad in nothing but his

shirt, I tiptoed out of his room.

* * *

Thad

I had just awakened, and the absence of Sera beside me puzzled me. A frown crept onto my face as I headed to the bathroom, still wondering about

her whereabouts.

As I showered, my thoughts churned about last night, one

of the most blissful nights I'd experienced, and I couldn't help but hope that she didn't regret it.

After my shower, I explored the house, searching for any sign of her presence,

but she was nowhere to be found. I emerged outside, where a refreshing

breeze greeted me.

There, I spotted her by the pool, her face illuminated by the soft glow of the morning sun. She was in hushed conversation on the phone, her whispered words barely audible.

I couldn't help but wonder, was it Senior on the line again?

My gaze drifted over her attire. She was dressed in a pair of shorts and a crop top, which accentuated her figure-the same body that I had run my hands over just yesterday, basking in the blissful sensation of having her all

to myself.

My desire for her surged once more as I made my way toward her, like a silent

specter, drawn to her allure. The gentle breeze tousled her hair, making it

look like she was filming for an advertisement.

"Mum, you know I can't come there now. Why don't you ask someone else?" she groaned, stomping her feet a little.

A smile curled on my lips when I

realized she was talking to her mum. An image of a short woman with green

eyes, just like Sera's, came to mind, although it was a bit blurry.

I walked over to her as she ended the call and wrapped my arms around her

waist, causing her to gasp in surprise.

"Morning," I whispered into her ear, planting a soft peck. She smiled and

turned her head slightly.

"Did you sleep well?" I asked, looking into her green eyes. She nodded with

a

sheepish grin.

I pulled away, taking her hand.

"Come on, we need to go somewhere," I said, already leading her along.

"Where?" She asked, her curiosity getting the best of her.

"You'll see," I replied, pulling her closer as we made our way into the house.

Seraphina

They say life can be wonderful when you're with the right person. That's

exactly how I felt as I laughed heartily when Thad playfully splashed water

on me.

He had insisted on a picnic, and we both cooked and packed pastries

to enjoy here by the water.

We spent the day reading novels, sketching each other, playing around, and now we were in the water, our antics making us look like a carefree couple.

"Come here," he said, pulling me closer by the arms and wrapping his wet hands around my waist.

His eyes shimmered as he gazed at me and whispered, "I love you, Sera."

I couldn't help but smile, unable to find the right words to respond. Instead, I

ruffled his wet hair, and water splashed around us, prompting a joyful chuckle

from us.

"What are your plans for the weekend?" Thad asked, his eyes fixed on mine.

We were seated on the grass, enjoying the scenic view of the sea and the

soothing sounds of the water.

I pondered for a moment. "I'm not sure yet. Why do you ask?" I began.

He interrupted, "I'd like to take you on a date."

My gaze shifted from the beautiful view to his face, where I found a soft smile

and his intense grey eyes locking onto mine.

"You always have your way, Thaddeus," I remarked, with a chuckle, my eyes

returning to the sea.

A hint of huskiness colored his voice as he replied, "I enjoy it when you call

me that."

"When I call you what?" I inquired, curious.

"My full name. It sounds intriguing when you say it," he continued, his eyes never leaving me.

I inched closer to him, cupping his face with my hands before kissing him tenderly. We pulled back, our eyes locked, and he swiftly pulled me in for another passionate kiss.

* * *

Thad

It had been days since my return from our Paris trip, and I'd never been happier. I was making the most of every moment, taking Sera on dates and showering her with flowers and gifts to express my affection.

My thoughts were interrupted by a soft knock on my office door, and Mark,

my assistant, walked in.

"Yes?" I inquired.

"Sir, Miss Callista is here to see you," he informed me.

"Let her in," I responded. Mark nodded and exited the room. I sighed, leaning

back in my chair, already having a sense of why Callista had come.

The door swung open, revealing a worried Callista who walked in, her red heels echoing on the tile floor and her fragrance enveloping my office.

"Are we even friends?" she questioned, her voice tinged with concern.

I knew Callista well, and one thing she couldn't stand was not being aware of my whereabouts.

"Callie," I began.

"You could have called or sent a message, but you did neither. I called your assistant several times, and he said you didn't have your personal phone with you. I was so scared," her voice trembled.

"Callie, I was on a business trip. I was swamped with work, and I should have

informed you about it," I replied with a sigh as I rose from my chair.

I couldn't help but wonder why she was more upset than usual.

"You were too busy taking a girl on a trip," she blurted out, her hazel eyes

fixed on me.

"That's none of your business, Callista," I responded, establishing my boundaries, surprised by her sudden change in tone and attitude.

She swallowed hard, realizing she probably shouldn't have said what she did.

"I'm sorry. I just..." Her voice trailed off. "I'll leave you to your work, Thad,"

she mumbled, then turned and walked out of my office.

I sank back into my chair with a sigh, displeased by the way our conversation

had concluded.

* * *

Seraphina

"So, what is it that you wanted to talk about?" I asked, setting my beer can

on the table and locking my gaze with his sapphire blue eyes.

Lys let out a slow breath and reached for my hands, gently squeezing them.

He looked deep into my eyes, determination and vulnerability in his expression.

"I know I should've said this a long time ago, and it might be too late now,

but... I like you, Sera. I like you a lot," he confessed, and I could sense the

courage it took to admit his feelings.

I felt a mix of shock and sympathy. Not because I hadn't sensed his attrac-
tion,

but because I was already committed to Thad.

"Lys, I..." I began to respond, but he interrupted me.

"Please, let me finish. I've rehearsed this a hundred times," he said with a

slightly awkward chuckle. "I would really appreciate it if you'd give me a

chance to prove myself, even if it's just once." I paused, considering his
words, and gently withdrew my hands from his

grasp.

"Lys, I like you too, as a friend, and nothing more. I'm... I have a boyfriend,"
I confessed, stumbling over my words.

His eyes widened in surprise and confusion.

"But I've never seen any guy around you," he whispered, searching my face.

"Is it..."

"Yes, it's him," I confirmed, already knowing he was referring to Thad.

"You told me he was just someone you knew," he said, as if questioning my honesty.

"I didn't lie. It just sort of... happened. Remember the guy from my past I told you about?" I inquired, and he nodded slowly.

"It's him. His name is Thad, and I love him. I love him so much, and he's the one I want to be with," I revealed, the words escaping my lips almost unexpectedly.

"What if he's playing you? What if he hurts you?" Lys voiced his concerns, his worry evident.

"No, he won't. I know Thad, and he's not like that," I replied with conviction.

"People can change, Sera," he whispered, sounding troubled.

I sighed, feeling apologetic. "I'm really sorry, Lys, but..."

A small, understanding smile crossed his face. "It's okay. You said you love him, and that's what matters most-your happiness," he began. "I guess I should've acted sooner instead of wasting time."

I managed a smile in response.

"But you can at least give me a hug, right?" he asked. I nodded and embraced him tightly.

I had just changed into shorts and a comfy T-shirt when my doorbell rang.

A quick glance at the wall clock showed it was already past 9 PM. Lys had left

a while ago, and I was puzzled about the unexpected visitor as Clara hadn't

given me any heads up.

Speaking of Clara, she'd been relentless with her questions about Thad, and Iwas growing tired of the constant explanations.

Wondering who might be at the door, I approached cautiously and peeked through the peephole. A tall figure came into view, and I couldn't help butsmile.

Chapter 21

S eraphina

Opening the door wide, I found Thad standing there with yet another bouquet of flowers, his favorite gift to surprise me with. I half-joked to myself about tarting a flower garden in my home.

"Hey," he greeted warmly, pulling me into a comforting hug. "I've missed you

so much, especially your scent," he whispered as he nuzzled my neck, sending delightful shivers down my spine.

"I brought you this," he said, handing me the bouquet, and I accepted it with a warm grin before ushering him inside and closing the door behind us.

In the living room, Thad had taken off his coat and made himself comfortable

on the couch. I headed to my room to place the flowers in a vase before

quickly returning.

"It's quite chilly outside. Would you like me to make some tea?" I asked as

I entered the kitchen. Gathering the necessary items, I started preparing a

warm drink.

I called out to him, "Thad!" but when I turned around, he stood right behind

me.

"No, what I want is you," he whispered in a husky voice, his eyes now intense

and alluring. He pulled me closer by my neck and kissed me passionately.

He swiftly moved his hands to my thighs, lifting me up slightly, and pressed my back against the fridge. I circled my arms around his neck, fingers weaving through his hair.

"I thought you were tired," I managed to mumble, my breath coming out in

ragged pants as he trailed kisses along my neck.

"Not when it comes to you," he whispered, his voice laden with desire.

He carefully unzipped my shorts, his fingers sliding down the zipper.

Simultaneously, he unzipped his own pants.

"Don't tell me you're planning to have your way with me against the fridge Thaddeus," I whispered as he gently put me down and removed my shorts.

"Watch me," he whispered in response, turning me around so my back was

against the fridge.

I held onto the fridge for support as he left a trail of kisses down my face.

His hand moved slowly towards my panties, caressing the area around it.

He gradually removed my panties, his gaze locked on me as I breathed

heavily, my eyes fixed on him.

With my panties now flung aside, he slid his fingers inside me, gently pumping them in and out. I was incredibly wet, feeling his fingers effortlessly glide in and out of me.

"Thad, wait..." I whispered, but he paid no heed. He took hold of one of my exposed thighs and knelt down, pulling it over his shoulder.

His tongue traced a path from my knee to my most sensitive spot. It fluttered up and down my slit, and then he flicked my clit with his tongue. I let out another gasp, my legs quivering as he persistently licked and sucked on my clit. My hands found their way into his hair, pulling him closer as I gasped in pure pleasure.

He ceased his attention on my clit and gently inserted a finger into my wetness. He gradually worked it in and out a few times before adding a second finger.

I continued to moan loudly in pleasure, gripping the fridge for support.

Suddenly, he stopped and stood up, then guided me towards the kitchen counter. My legs shook noticeably as I made my way there.

He turned me around and positioned me face down.

"Oh my goodness!" I gasped as I felt the head of his shaft pressing against

my rear entrance. He inched forward, and a soft moan escaped my lips as he

entered me.

His hands firmly gripped my hips as he began to thrust in and out of me.

I clutched the counter for support, my cheeks resting on the cool, smooth

surface.

I could hear his breath quickening, growing faster and deeper. He let out

occasional grunts, punctuating his thrusts in and out.

My phone suddenly rang loudly on the kitchen counter where I had left it

earlier Thad," I whispered amidst our passionate encounter, "I have a call."

But he wasn't paying attention.

"Thad!" I said, raising my voice a little. He suddenly stopped and placed a

hand on my back, our heavy breathing filling the kitchen.

He withdrew and took a step back as I rushed to answer the phone, but it had

stopped ringing before I could pick it up.

I sighed and turned to look at him.

"I'm sorry," he said, his voice uncertain, trying to catch his breath. I could see

him zipping up his pants.

I let out a tired laugh.

* * *

"So what did I do to him?" Thad asked, stifling a laugh as he looked at me with a grin.

"What else? You punched him, and everyone gasped. I felt bad because it was my fault," I explained with hand gestures for emphasis.

We sat on my couch, munching on pizza and watching a movie he'd picked out. He wanted me to share some stories from his high school days, hoping to jog his memory.

"I just knew I'd do that," he said with a smirk, making me chuckle.

You were pretty clingy back then," I pointed out.

"I was?" he asked, raising an eyebrow.

"You couldn't sleep if I wasn't there," I said casually, noticing a hint of discomfort on his face.

He suddenly ran a hand through his hair and let out a groan.

"Thad? What's wrong? Are you okay?" I asked, concerned.

He stopped and looked at me, as if grappling with some inner turmoil.

"I'm fine," he whispered, "but... why did you lie in the first place?"

"What do you mean?"

"You knew me back then, and we dated. So why did you say you didn't know me? You kept it a secret," he questioned, his eyes filled with intensity.

I sighed, reluctant to reveal that his mother had warned me to stay away from him.

"I was just... scared you wouldn't like me anymore," I admitted, making up an excuse.

He was about to say more when my phone buzzed again, and I quickly

grabbed it, stepping away from him.

"Hello,"

"Chef Everhart," a familiar voice, resonated through the phone, causing my heart to race.

Chapter 22

I know it must be surprising for you to receive my call, Chef Everhart," Callista said, her gaze fixed on me.

The soft glow of the restaurant's lights highlighted her vibrant, red wavy hair, casting a warm aura around her.

"It is, and please, just call me Sera. Chef Everhart feels a bit too official," I replied, offering a friendly smile.

"Alright, Sera, no need for formalities. Let's get to the heart of the matter. What's your connection with Thad, and why did you decide to go on a trip with him?" Callista's tone shifted, a hint of curiosity and concern playing in her voice.

"What?" I asked, caught off guard by her statement.

"I can't believe this," she scoffed, her disbelief evident. "How can I come to your restaurant with a date, and a chef managed to sweep my date off his feet and go on a trip with him? Does any of this even make sense to you?" Her voice raised slightly, frustration in her tone.

I stared at her, my silence speaking volumes.

"You're just a chef Thad met in this restaurant, so whatever you have with him won't last long. But with me…" She paused, emphatically pointing to her own chest. "I mean, I'm everything to him. We've known each other since our college days."

"So, what are you getting at, Callista?" I asked, forgoing the "miss" in her name.

She sighed and leaned in closer. "I'm saying this for your own sake. Don't invest your time in Thad because he'll never choose you over me. He and I go way back," she whispered, her eyes locked onto mine.

A small smile curled up on my face as I regarded her with amusement.

"I'm glad Thad has had someone like you by his side all these years, someone who claims to know him inside and out," I said.

Her expression shifted to confusion. "Have you been keeping tabs on Thad, monitoring his whereabouts and the people he meets?" I inquired, my smile fading.

"That's none of your business," she replied in a hushed voice, realizing I had caught her.

"Callista, let me be direct. I'm not the type to fight over a guy. And you should know that I've known Thad for a long time, even before his college days. Right now, we're in a relationship," I paused, observing her reaction, which confirmed my expectations. Anger flickered across her face.

"I love him, and he loves me too. I don't believe I'm wasting my time with him," I continued. I stood up, leaned in closer, and whispered, "Have a nice day, Callista, and I'd appreciate it if you didn't call me for meetings like this. Ever again." With that, I turned and walked away from the restaurant, each step carrying a sense of finality.

Thad I stood a few steps away from Sera, both of us on a hill, gazing down at the breathtaking beauty of nature. She had insisted on this location, and I didn't question her reasons.

My feelings for her were unwavering, and she was the one I desired. The past no longer mattered; all I wanted was to be with her.

A gentle breeze rustled through her hair, and I couldn't help but smile as she tucked a loose strand behind her ear. Her actions only added to her charm.

I removed my coat, taking slow steps toward her, and then gently wrapped it around her shoulders, ensuring she was properly covered.

I wrapped my arms around Sera, leaning in close to nuzzle her neck and inhaling her familiar, delightful strawberry scent. It was a fragrance I had grown to love.

"Do you like it?" I whispered, to which she nodded.

"My mum wants to meet you, Sera," I mentioned, releasing my embrace and standing beside her.

She gazed up at me, her eyes reflecting a mixture of shock and a hint of fear.

"My mum is not a hard person to please. She's genuinely nice," I added with a light chuckle, aware of her nerves.

"Why does she want to see me?" She asked, her green eyes sparkling in the night.

"Because you're my girlfriend, and she's eager to meet you," I stated plainly. Sera diverted her gaze, looking ahead.

" I am sure you knew my mum in the past?" I asked hesitantly.

"Very well," she whispered and turned to me, mustering a forced smile. "I did everything I could ever think of doing with your mum, Thad. We cooked, danced, laughed, and even went shopping together."

"Oh…" I responded, taken aback by this revelation.

"It will be nice to meet her again, though," she said, trying to ease the tension.

I nodded in agreement and took her right hand, squeezing it gently.

"It's fine if you don't want to meet her now; we can always postpone it," I reassured her, trying to warm her cold hands in mine.

"No. I can't run away forever, Thad. I'll have to meet her eventually," she whispered.

"What do you mean?" I asked, puzzled.

"Nothing," she replied, shaking her head slightly. "Why are you no longer curious to know about your past and what really happened?"

"Why should I?" I questioned.

"Thad… you were already regaining your memories, and they suddenly stopped coming to you. Aren't you curious to know more about our past?"

"No. I'm not. Not anymore, anyway. I mean…" I paused, pulling her closer to me. "You're with me now, and there's nothing more I need to know," I whispered, planting a soft kiss on her right cheek.

She gazed at me as if she wanted to say something but stopped, offering a warm smile.

"I love you," I whispered and pulled her into a loving hug.

"So, do you mind telling me more about your senior friend, the guy who always seems to be around you?" I asked, pulling away slightly.

"What do you mean? Senior friend? He's just a friend, haven't we talked about this before?" She replied with a brief laugh.

"I don't like him getting too close to you. He seems obsessed with you, Sera, and it worries me," I confessed.

She playfully smacked my chest. "No, you're the one who's obsessed with me."

A sense of déjà vu washed over me as I looked at her smiling face.

"You're so obsessed with her. Why are you going to find her at this hour? It's late, Thaddeus," a voice echoed in my head.

"Thad? Thad?" Sera's voice brought me back from my thoughts.

"Huh?" I mumbled, shaking off the reverie.

"Are you okay?" She inquired, and I nodded quickly.

"What about you? Callista clearly has feelings for you, and I'm sure she still visits your office," she probed.

"No, she doesn't. I told her not to come since you didn't like it," I admitted.

She pouted slightly and turned away from me, heading toward the car with long strides.

"Where are you going?" I asked, laughing softly as I followed her.

"Somewhere away from you, you're lying," she retorted, her voice rising with a tinge of jealousy.

A smile crept onto my lips as I caught up with her.

Chapter 23

I released a shaky breath as the familiar door swung open, and I followed Thad inside, his grip on my hand firm and reassuring.

I glanced around the house, noting the significant changes that had taken place, which made everything feel a bit strange to me.

We eventually made our way to the garden, and there she was—the woman I hadn't laid eyes on in years. She was deeply engrossed in ensuring the food was served correctly, so she didn't notice us approaching.

"Mom," Thad called out. She looked up from her tasks and fixed her gaze on us.

"I know I mentioned I was bringing my girlfriend, and you may have met before in the past. This is Sera," he introduced, glancing briefly in my direction.

I offered a small smile as I looked at Vivienne, a flood of memories from that fateful night in the hospital rushing back to me.

Vivienne's once-black hair now featured a few strands of white, adding to her beauty. Her grey eyes still sparkled, much like Thad's.

Shock overtook her face as she gazed at me. "Vivienne," I croaked out.

Her eyes shifted to Thad, and the shock morphed into anger.

"Why didn't you tell me you were bringing her here, Thad? You can't bring her here," she declared, her voice harsh, and it felt like a blow to my face.

"Mum... What do you mean?" Thad inquired, confusion evident.

"I thought I explicitly told you to stay away from my son, Seraphina. I will never allow you two to be together," she said, shifting her gaze to me.

I swallowed hard, expecting this reaction.

"You told her not to approach me?" Thad questioned, pulling his hands away from mine and walking closer to his mother.

"She's a danger to you, Thad. She shouldn't be here," his mom yelled. My heart raced as memories rushed back to me.

"Now I know the voice in my head was yours, Mum. You were the one who said I was obsessed with her?" Thad said.

"Yes, I did say that. And I didn't lie. Do you know what she did to you?" his mom retorted.

"I don't care anymore!" Thad yelled, his anger becoming increasingly apparent in the midst of this tense situation.

"She caused your accident, she's the reason you had that accident and lost half of your memories. You missed your high school graduation, and you were in a coma for months. She's not fit to be in your life anymore. I won't allow someone like her near you," his mother accused vehemently.

Thad stared at her in shock.

"I... I don't care about my accident anymore, Mum. Sera is the person I love, and I'm not leaving her," he insisted.

"Well, you can continue, but I won't accept her into this house," she declared, turning her attention to me. "Aren't you ashamed, Sera? After having my son wrapped around your finger all through high school, causing him to lose his memory, and now you come back to claim him, huh?" She shouted.

"Mom, stop it! I won't let you talk to her like that," Thad protested.

I released a shaky breath, feeling a raw nerve had been touched.

"She's right, Thad," I began, looking up at him. He turned to meet my gaze.

"I... I caused your accident that night, and..." I faltered, unable to control my emotions. "I'm sorry for coming here, Vivienne," I whispered, turning and making a hasty exit from the garden.

"Sera!" Thad's voice called out as he followed me, but I broke into a run, trying to escape. "Sera, stop running!" Thad's voice echoed behind me as he pursued me.

I had taken a taxi from his house, and he was following me with his car. Guilt and regret weighed heavily on my heart for everything that had transpired.

I berated myself for believing I deserved Thad again, especially after running away when he needed me most. Allowing him to have his way with me multiple times, even though I knew I didn't deserve him, was a mistake. I shouldn't have let him back into my life, gone on the trip, or—

I cried out as I continued to run down an unfamiliar, dark path. A strong hand seized my arm, yanking me around to face Thad.

I stared back at Thad's furious expression. "You should stay away from me," i shrieked, tears streaming down my face as I jerked my arm from his grip, moving away.

"Is that what you think, too? Like my mom? How could you let our relationship crumble because of her words?" Thad yelled, his voice laden with pain.

"Because she's right. Everything is my fault. I should've stayed away from you, just as I've been doing," I yelled back, my chest heaving. "I... shouldn't have let myself love you again. I had no right," I whispered, hot tears trailing down my face.

"I don't care... I don't. How many times do I have to say it for you to understand?" Thad groaned, approaching me.

"Please, stop, Thad. I care because you don't. I do, because I'm to blame here," I said, taking a step back, causing him to halt.

"Sera, you're hurting me," he whispered, his eyes locked on me. I saw tears welling up in his eyes, the same ones from the night of his accident.

My heart ached as I watched him.

"Don't cry for me, Thad. Please don't. I should've answered your call that night, and none of this would have happened," I admitted.

A solitary tear slid down his face as he stared at me.

"If you're thinking of leaving me, Sera, you need to discard that foolish notion now," he insisted. "Let's just... go home," he added, his voice filled with desperation.

"I..." I started to reply when I noticed a figure behind him, holding a large object in his hand.

"Thad!" I yelled, making my way toward him, but he was a fraction of a second too late. The object struck his head hard.

Thad collapsed to the ground, his head slamming against the floor. I let out a piercing scream, my eyes fixed on the assailant.

The man with disheveled dark hair, dressed in all black, approached me and forcibly yanked me away from Thad.

"Is he your little boyfriend?" He sneered into my ear as I struggled to free myself from his grip. His hold on my hair was unyielding.

"Thad!" I cried out, my gaze still fixed on Thad lying on the floor. His eyes were closed, and he wasn't moving.

Fear coursed through me as the man began dragging me towards the path I had taken when Thad chased me.

"No... wait... you can't leave him like that!" I pleaded, attempting to reach Thad.

"Shut the fuck up!" he shouted, pulling me forcefully with him.

A car suddenly pulled up, and two men stepped out, sprinting toward us with guns in their hands.

"Mr. Tate!" one of them called, aiming his gun at us.

The man with me brandished a knife, pressing it against my neck, his other hand still gripping my hair. My head throbbed, and dizziness overcame me as things spiraled out of control.

"Stay away from me, or I'll slice her to pieces!" he threatened, pulling me back.

I groaned in pain, my hand still on his, desperately trying to free myself from his grip.

"Okay, okay," the men, presumably the police, conceded, placing their guns on the ground.

Seizing the opportunity, I struck him hard with my elbow in his chest, causing him to stumble backward.

I turned and rushed toward Thad, but the sharp sound of a gunshot echoed, freezing me in my tracks.

Chapter 24

P^{ast}

I emerged from the bathroom, my hand throbbing from repeatedly striking thebathroom mirror. Blood oozed from the cuts on my hand.

Staring at the ring in my hand, I decided to remove it and place it in a drawer. Guilt gnawed at me as I noticed that her luggage was no longer there. I had wrongly accused her, and now she was gone.

I picked up my car keys and phone, heading out of our room. The thought of finding Sera consumed me.

"Where are you going?" my mother's voice interrupted me as I descended the stairs, dialing Sera's phone.

"To find Sera," I replied, walking toward the door.

"Thad!" My mother's call halted me, and I turned to look at her.

"What's going on? You're so obsessed with her. Why are you going to find herat this hour? It's late, Thaddeus," my mother chided, her voice gaining a touch of concern.

I glanced at the time on my phone and realized it was just a few minutes shy of 9PM.

"I'll be back, Mom. I promise I won't stay too long," I assured her, rushing out the door.

As I sped down the road with an anxious heart, I dialed Sera's phone, hoping she'd answer.

"Please, pick up," I whispered under my breath, my eyes glued to the screen in my car.

Glancing up, I noticed I was nearing Sera's house. But before I could react, a sudden, violent collision rocked my car, sending it into a chaotic spin. My head felt muddled, and all I could do was brace myself for the impending impact.

My car tumbled repeatedly before finally coming to a crashing halt. Pain coursed through me, and I winced as shards of glass embedded themselves in my face.

Struggling to release my seatbelt became an agonizing task, and my body felt immobilized.

The car's door was forcibly yanked open, and I heard the hushed murmurs of people nearby. Two men quickly dragged me from the wreck, and the cold night air washed over my face.

Lying on my back, I gazed up at the night sky, my vision beginning to blur.

"Thad!" a voice cried out with urgency, and approaching footsteps followed. A

familiar scent enveloped me, and I gradually opened my eyes to find those green eyes staring down at me.

"Don't leave me alone," I managed to croak.

"I won't..." her voice trailed off as darkness closed in around me.

Present

I slowly opened my eyes, initially hearing muffled sounds before the voices became clearer. Expecting to see those green eyes, I was met with grey ones filled with concern.

"Thaddeus, can you hear me?" my mother's voice inquired as she leaned over me. She turned to address someone else. "He's awake, call the doctor."

I let out a soft groan, shifting my head to the right, and realized I was in a hospital.

"Mum," I croaked.

"Yes? Do you need water?" She inquired and promptly moved to get water from a large jug.

"Here," she said, offering a cup of water. She pressed a button, causing my bed to rise slightly.

I took the cup and eagerly drank the water.

"Where is she?" I managed to utter as she took the cup from me.

"Who?"

"Where is Sera?" I questioned, my eyes scanning my private ward.

Seraphina I set the phone down and settled onto the couch, letting out a relieved sigh.

My gaze wandered around my packed luggage, and I stood up, preparing to unpack them. It had been several days since the incident when I unintentionally led Thad into danger by running into that dark path. Seanhad just informed me that Thad had woken up from his coma.

I couldn't muster the strength to go back to him. The moment his mother-arrived at the hospital, I had fled. I sighed as I pulled my bag out. I had made up my mind; I would not approach Thad again. His mother was right - being with me always seemed to bring danger to him.

Leaving Thad when I loved him so deeply tore at my heart. I longed to see his face, to be by his side, but it felt like my only option was to stay away from him.

My phone chimed, and I picked it up, answering with a shaky voice, "Hello."

"Seraphina, this is not how I raised you. How could you pack up and leave your apartment without informing me? I'm in your house right now, and they told me you've gone," my mother scolded, her voice rising in anger.

"Mum..." I whispered before my sobs overtook me.

Thad

"It's the same man," Sean's voice came through the phone, sounding somber.

I let out a heavy sigh. "Alright, thanks, Sean," I responded before ending thecall. It had been two weeks since I woke up, and I remained in the dark aboutSera's whereabouts.

I had gone to her house, only to find it deserted. She'd even left her job at the restaurant, and her friend had clammed up about her location. Sera had ceased contacting Sean, and her phone was switched off. Since her departure, I'd been spiraling into a deep emotional turmoil, unable to find my equilibrium.

I raked my hands through my hair, my frustration evident, and pushed awayfrom my chair to walk over to the window.

A knock on my door interrupted my thoughts, and Mark entered, holdinghis usual notepad.

"Yes?" I inquired in a wearied tone.

"A woman named Clara is here to see you," he informed me. My eyes widenedslightly, and my heart quickened its pace.

"Let her in," I said quickly.

Seraphina

I closed the supermarket's door behind me and slipped my phone into myjacket pocket. In my other hand, I carried a polyethylene nylon filled withbeer.

As I strolled down the street, I gazed up at the night sky, marveling at thestars' beauty.

"Beautiful," I whispered to myself before redirecting my attention ahead.

My new apartment was just a few meters away, and I was almost there when my phone buzzed. I retrieved it, and a faint smile appeared on my face.

"Senior," I exhaled.

"How are you finding your new place?" he inquired.

"It's really peaceful, and the surroundings are quite inviting. I love it," I replied, my gaze lowered as I continued my walk.

We chatted for a few more minutes, but as I raised my eyes, I spotted a loomingfigure outside my house. No need for a security camera; I recognized him by his imposing stature, the large grey coat he wore, and the intensity of his grey eyes as they locked onto me in the darkness.

My heart raced as I approached him, stopping a few steps away.

"Senior, let me call you back," I whispered, abruptly ending the call, my gaze fixed firmly on his face.

His expression remained stoic, and beneath the dim streetlight's glow, I could discern the weariness in his eyes and the fatigue etched on his features.

"What are you doing here?" I inquired.

"Is that really the first thing you're going to say to me, Seraphina? After leaving me twice?" he retorted, his tone harsh.

"It's for your own good. Now, please leave," I replied, attempting to pass him, but he swiftly caught my hand, causing me to meet his gaze.

"You're incredibly cruel, Sera," he whispered, his breath chilling my face inthe cold night.

"How could you contemplate doing this to me all over again? That night of the accident, you could have stayed with me, but you left before I even wokeup," he murmured.

"And you're doing the same thing. Do you ever consider how I would feelwithout you by my side? I..." he trailed off, releasing his grip on me.

"It's clear you don't care about me. Not once have you ever said you loved mewhen we were together," he accused.

"I did, in the past," I interjected.

"That was in the past, and the past is gone, forever. This is the present, Sera.Why do you keep dwelling on the past?" he yelled, his voice filled with frustration.

Tears welled up in my eyes as I gazed at him, unable to speak.

"Tell me, Sera, do you love me?" he pleaded, his eyes searching mine. A flash of the night of the accident surfaced in my mind; he had asked me the same question then.

"I..." I faltered, my voice trembling. "You should go, Thad," I whispered, turning my gaze away from his face, not wanting him to witness the tears about to escape.

"If you enter that house, I'll take it as your way of breaking up with me andwanting nothing to do with me," he whispered, his stare unwavering.

"Haven't I made that clear already?" I retorted sharply, then proceeded towalk past him as tears streamed down my face.

I shut the door behind me and sank to the floor, my sobs resonating throughthe empty house. The thought of losing Thad forever consumed me. The pain was unbearable; I might never see him again.

My anguish took hold as I clutched my hair tightly, infuriated by my ownactions. I hadn't meant to speak to him that way or treat him like that.

Everything I did was out of love, yet it had resulted in the opposite of what Ihad wanted.

I cried for a few more minutes, my heart aching, but then determination surged within me. I couldn't bear to lose him, not after all we had gone through.

I yanked the door open and rushed outside, only to be greeted by an emptystreet. A soft sob escaped my lips as I began to run, unsure of whether I should go left or right.

"Thad!" I screamed as I sprinted down the right road.

I ran desperately, searching for Thad everywhere, but he remained out ofsight. My eyes were puffy from crying, and my feet hurt from all the running.

Approaching a nearby park, I hurried inside. Couples all around wereshowing affection, but I paid them no attention. Finding Thad was all thatmattered.

Then, I spotted a familiar grey coat draped over a bench. Someone sat there with their head down, buried in their hands.

I came to a stop, breathing heavily, my hair sticking to my sweaty face. My heart raced as I approached the figure.

When I stood right in front of him, he lifted his head, a look of surprise on his face as he saw me.

I hastily enveloped him in a tight hug, burying my face in his neck while my tears flowed freely. His cologne surrounded me, familiar and comforting.

"I'm so sorry. I didn't mean any of what I said. I love Thaddeus, I love you somuch that it hurts to leave you. ," I confessed through my muffled sobs against his neck.

I felt his hands wrap around me gently, patting my back in a soothing manner.

"You scared the hell out of me, Sera," he whispered, returning the hug tightly.

Epilogue

I slowly opened my eyes, and there he was, my husband, Thaddeus Whitlock,

his handsome face turned toward me as he slept. His eyes were peacefully

closed, and he looked like a child in slumber.A soft smile graced my lips as I ran my fingers through his hair, causing him

to let out a little groan in his sleep. Gently, I brushed a few strands of his hair away from his face.I slid the blankets off my legs, revealing my naked body, and took a deep

breath. Memories of our honeymoon here in Paris flooded my mind.

Thad had been doting on me, treating me like I was the most precious thing in the world, and he couldn't keep his hands off me.With a sense of contentment, I rose from the bed and reached for his white

shirt, which I had playfully ripped off his chest the previous night. I draped it

over my body before heading into the bathroom.I let out a groan as I prepared coffee in the kitchen. Thad had developed a morning coffee ritual during our honeymoon, and I knew he'd be joining me soon.

My mother had been urging me to come back home and take a pregnancytest, not understanding that Thad wanted our honeymoon to continue."Your honeymoon is almost a month long now, Sera. Anyway, let me know

when you come back home, okay?" She said before ending the call.Sighing, I looked at my phone's screen and felt a pair of strong arms wrap

around my waist. I turned to see Thad, bare-chested, smiling down at me.

His eyes were still half-closed, a sign that he had just woken up."Good morning," I whispered, then kissed him softly."Is that coffee for me?" He asked as soon as I pulled away, his eyes on the

steaming cup.I nodded and handed it to him. He took a sip and then set it down on the

counter."Shall we get back to work now?" He asked, taking my hand."What kind of work is that?" I asked, already knowing the answer."The one we couldn't finish last night because you complained that your thigh was sore," he replied matter-of-factly."Thad, it's still sore," I fibbed."You can't fool me, Seraphina. My mother is pressuring me, and so is yours," he said, then effortlessly scooped me up in his arms. I gasped and wrapped my arms around his neck."It's already past 9 am, Thad," I pointed out as he carried me towards the

bedroom.

Who cares?" He said, using his foot to open the door as we entered the room.